I0531612

As the Heavens Smiled

The story of three inseparable friends
and the destiny that binds them

Hassan Asghar Bhatti

Absolute Author
Publishing House

As the Heavens Smiled
Copyright © 2020 by Hassan Asghar Bhatti
ALL RIGHTS RESERVED

All rights reserved. No part of this publication may be reproduced, distributed, or transmitted in any form or by any means, including photocopying, recording, or other electronic or mechanical methods, without the prior written permission of the AUTHOR, except in the case of brief quotations embodied in critical reviews and certain other noncommercial uses permitted by copyright law. This is a work of fiction. Names, characters, businesses, places, events, locales, and incidents are either the products of the author's imagination or used in a fictitious manner. Any resemblance to actual persons, living or dead, or actual events is purely coincidental.

Publisher: Absolute Author Publishing House
Editor: Dr. Melissa Caudle

LIBRARY OF CONGRESS CATALOGUE IN-PUBLICATION-DATA

As the Heavens Smiled/ Hassan Asghar Bhatti

      p. cm.

ISBN: 978-1-64953-064-6

1. Fiction   2. Suspense

DEDICATED

To

Mian Murad Asghar Bhatti

My mentor in everything I know

and

Paras, Fatima, Fateh, and Ayat

ACKNOWLEDGMENT

I have been thinking about writing for a long time now, and finally, I took the step forward and wrote my debut book, which you are about to read. It was not only me and my writing that made it possible there were a lot of people who stood by me in this endeavor.

First of all, I would like to thank my publisher and editor, Dr. Melissa Caudle, without her trust in me, this would not have been possible.

Secondly, I would like to thank my parents Mian Zahid Hussain Bhatti and Nuzhat Jabeen, who always encouraged me to do whatever I want to without their unconditional support. I could not have taken this step.

I want to thank my sister Noor and my cousin Naqi who put up with me through this journey and beta read my work and gave me feedback and suggestions on how to improve this book.

I want to thank the people who inspired me to write a book of my own, and among those people are Mr. Mohsin Hamid, Mr. Omar Shahid Hamid, Mr. Mohammad Hanif, Miss Fatima Bhutto, Mr. Chetan Bhagat, and last but not least, Mr. Paulo Coehlo. These are a few of my favorite authors out there, and I have read all their books. It is because of these great authors that genuinely inspired me to write.

And Lastly, I want to thank all my friends and family who supported me through this journey with an unmeasurable encouragement.

TABLE OF CONTENTS

Hassan Asghar Bhatti

Epigraph

Three Small Poems ~ *Karle Wilson Baker*

I will spread out my mind
As the wind spreads the skies:
I will make my heart Argus, Full of love's eyes:
So shall I grow Abysmally wise.

MEEKNESS AND PRIDE

Meekness and Pride Are fruits of one tree: Eat of them both
For mastery:
Take one of Pride —
Of the other,
three.

COURAGE

Courage is armor
A blind man wears;
The calloused scar of outlived despairs: Courage is fear
That has said its prayers

As the Heavens Smiled

Prologue

The campus was abuzz with rumors about what had happened last month -- few students, well-known and well-liked around campus, went missing. The events around their disappearances were jumbled, and no two stories about what could have happened seemed to line up.

A chill filled the air, and a light morning fog covered the wide-campus grounds and parking lots. The air smelled vaguely of flowers, mostly roses with a hint of jasmine. The Evergreen shrubbery trimmed to perfection in Boxwood hedges and an occasionally hidden figurine that the campus' groundkeeper had cut in a moment of impulsiveness lined the roads.

The autumn leaves danced as the light cool breeze swept them up into small tornadoes as they tumbled along the brick-paved walkways. The last of the summer flowers lingered as the change in season turned everything toward the shades of autumn. The greens, of spring and summer, surrendered to the bright reds, oranges, golds, and yellows of autumn. Few stray leaves held on stubbornly to their summer colours as everything surrounding them embraced the coming of autumn and the change of season.

The lovely picture the campus presented stood in stark juxtaposition against the general mood around campus. People in every corner could be seen whispering, talking about the events that had taken place just weeks earlier. The buzz and chatter of the students was almost deafening.

Everyone seemed to be talking about the same thing -- the whereabouts of Ahmed, Adnan, and Liyana? The details were obscure; in fact, the exact events were an unknown factor as well. The only thing that could be agreed upon was that all three of the students had met a rather unfortunate incident at the same time. The three best friends had been missing for a week now, and no one, not even their families, seemed to know what had happened to them.

Hassan Asghar Bhatti

Chapter One

Heads turned as they saw two young men run past, shouting at each other. Bystanders rolled their eyes as they saw a familiar scene play out before them. Adnan and Ahmed, the two boys who lived in one of the houses on the street, were often seen making a mad dash early in the morning toward the university. They were always late, running across the campus from the parking lot in a bid to make it to their lectures on time.

Adnan, the shorter of the two and older by two years at twenty-three, always ran ahead, while Ahmed played catch up in his mad dash attempt but fell behind periodically. Today, he managed to hold his own.

The boys ran along the main road speeding along the walkways as cars, motorcycles, wagons, and your occasional horse-drawn carriage zipped past them.

"Run! Move Adnan!! Dammit, bro; we're running late!" the taller boy shouted toward his running companion. He glanced to his side with a laugh as he saw his friend beside him.

Adnan gave him a smirk, and with a laugh, shouted back. The tall boy was a brunette, his hair resembling that of a dark jump rope; it gleamed almost chestnut in the bright midday sun. His shorter friend had stark black hair, so dark it almost glinted blue.

"I'm clearly moving faster than you! Pick up some slack, would you?" The wind carried his voice as he ran ahead of Ahmed. Then, the other increased his pace and ran alongside him once again. The back and forth continued between them as they neared the entrance for the computer department.

"You know you both are useless, right?" a female voice declared. The tone was filled with amusement, and that fact further illustrated by the smile on her face as if mocking them.

A young girl stood at the door; her hip cocked as

she held the door in place so her friends could bolt in. Upon seeing the girl

waiting, the guys slowed as they came to a halt, panting and gasping.

"You do know that today's lecture was moved to the afternoon, right?" Liyana asked. She watched as their expressions crumbled in disbelief, and the accusation on their faces made her burst out in a fit of uncontrolled laughter. Her laughter was rather pleasant to hear, light and airy, almost childlike. It lacked the self-consciousness and cynicism that often came with age.

Adnan collapsed on the ground in a heap with a loud laugh. "Talk about wasted effort! You could have texted us! Do you know how far we ran to be able to make it on time?" he complained, but it was all in good humor, evidenced by his smile.

"Do you even have to ask? You know she takes a perverse pleasure from watching us suffer. Right? She probably didn't tell us so she could watch us struggle," Ahmed declared, as he curled at the waist and bent his knees slightly while he took slow heaving breaths. He looked up at Liyana's smiling face, squinted in the light, still a bit hungover from last night. The bright sunlight stung his eyes as he tried to get his bearings. As usual, he took a moment to admire Liyana.

She looked striking, as always. She had her hair up in one of those messy buns on the top of her head and the short and long tendrils that had escaped and were framing her face beautifully. She always had a look about her. Messy but beautiful, like it was completely effortless for her. Sometimes Ahmed was in awe of her. She could laugh and fool around with them without being self- conscious at all.

Maybe it was because they had known each other for so long, but at times Ahmed wondered if Liyana ever saw him as a man, or even as someone of the opposite gender. It was hard to tell if his presence ever moved her, or if she was utterly immune to his masculine charm. She had this way of disarming him, and at some point, he wasn't sure when, but he started to feel like a gangly giraffe around her. He was never sure if he was saying the right words or doing the right things.

Their friendship in the last few years made him felt that he was walking on eggshells around her. He didn't want to jeopardize the relationship they had. They had been friends since they were kids and grew up around each other, witnessing all the awkward growth spurts, the heartbreaks, and the failed relationships over the years.

They didn't have any secrets from each other -- all but one. Ahmed was in love with her since he was twelve and had come to the startling realization that most boys probably arrive at much earlier in their lives that his best friend was a girl. Before that, it hadn't seemed like that much of a big deal.

For a moment, he was pulled back into the memory as he looked at how much Liyana had changed from the adorably awkward ten-year-old into this beautiful, funny, and loving young woman. It was hard to imagine that she was always horsing around with Ahmed and Adana as one of the boys when she had been younger.

***

Nine Years Ago

They had been running around playing in Adnan's garden. The garden had been filled with so many different colored flowers that the kids often made it a game to see who could spot the most. Adana's mother loved to be in the garden, and it was rather obvious from how well-tended that garden always was maintained. Jumping on the *charpai* and trying to play freeze tag at some point during all this running about, Adnan's father had stepped out into the garden to watch them horseplay.

As he had tackled Liyana to the ground in an attempt to freeze her in the game, he had heard Adnan's dad make this strange noise. It was something between a shout and just pure surprise.

"No! No! Ahmed! What are you doing? You can't play like that with a girl!" his voice moved nearer as he came around from his spot on the veranda toward them. He gently lifted them both up from the grass. He intently inspected Liyana for any injuries, only bothering to give a brief cursory look toward Ahmed from the corner of his eye.

"Liyana, are you okay? Did you get hurt?" He turned her around and inspected her knees and elbows for scrapes.
Ahmed and Adnan found his treatment of her absurdly funny. They couldn't understand why it was forbidden to play rough. They had been doing it for years, and no one had ever said anything about treating girls differently.

At some point, Adana's dad had sent Liyana inside so that he could talk to the boys alone. At the time, Ahmed had been angry at Adana's dad. It was just

6

like an adult to interrupt a perfectly good game and then pretend there was an incredibly good-adult reason for doing so.

He had begun to talk to them about how girls needed to be taken care off and how they more delicate than boys and seeing as that they were not only boys but also older than Liyana and it was their job to make sure she was taken care of and that she did not get hurt.

"Girls just aren't as strong as boys. You need to be careful around them. If they get hurt, it could be horrible, and..." Ahmed cut him off.

"...That's not true! Liyana is very strong. She can beat Adana and me when we are catching frogs, and she's not even a little scared of them. Besides, she's the fastest in our class; faster than all the girls and the boys!!! No one can beat her in a race and... and..." In his anger and hurry to defend Liyana, Ahmed became so worked up that he could no longer remember what he wanted to say. All he knew was that Adana's dad was wrong and that he was angry at him for making it sound like Liyana was not as good as them because she was a girl. Next thing he knew, he was tackled to the ground by a flimsy wisp of pink linen and hair.

It was Liyana. She had run out and grabbed him in a tight hug, her frock flying everywhere in the light breeze that had picked up since she was told to go inside. Her hair came undone from her braid, and the mass of light brown waives flew in all directions.

She hadn't said anything. Liyana wasn't someone who talked a lot, even as a child. Ahmed knew her well, and her behavior meant she was grateful. She was happy about the fact that Ahmed stood up for her. She didn't need to be grateful; Ahmed would always be there for her.

It took him a moment to realise that what he was feeling in his little twelve-year-old heart, that fluttering, that rapid beating of his heart, was, in fact, love.

It might sound foolish to some people considering that he was only twelve, but at that moment, Ahmed knew. He just knew that he loved her, and he would probably love her forever.

He didn't need adults telling him what he was feeling was foolish or stupid. He had never felt this way before, but this was the way his mother had once talked about his father, in her more vulnerable moments when she was telling the truth, and this was precisely how she had described feeling when she realised that she was in love with him.

However, Ahmed felt a moment of panic. What if, just like his mother, the person he was in love with didn't love him back? Or worse, what if Liyana hated him for telling her how he felt and ruining their friendship?

He could never tell her how he felt. If he did, he risked losing her. For him, he would rather spend his whole life loving her from afar than risk losing her because he was selfish.

***

"Oyye? Ahmed, are you there? You look like you've drifted off into the abyss. What are you thinking about so carefully?" Liyana stood in before him waving her hand in his face trying to get his attention. He had drifted off into the memory of nine years ago.

With a startled shake of his head, he smiled at her.

"Nothing, it's just... I don't know, I was thinking about the fact that I no longer have an afternoon free to nap in, that's all." He wanted to change the topic. Sometimes he thought Liyana could read his mind. It wouldn't be that bad, and maybe then he wouldn't always have to think about the fact that he was hiding something from her. Sometimes he wondered if she could tell he was hiding something, but he doubted that she could ever guess what it was.

"How about I'll buy you guys some breakfast. You can drink some coffee to wake up and please tell me you finished the assignment for this class. You know the one you were running here to attend." Liyana gathered her things from the ground where she had placed them while she waited for them.

"Oh no!" Adana groaned. "There was an assignment! What assignment? Damn it; why can't I remember. Ugh!" Adana walked off moaning as he contemplated how he was going to get his work done before the class this afternoon.

Depending on what it was, maybe he could get away with it. He just needed to scrape by with a 'C,' and then he could move on from this class. Truth be told, Adana wasn't all that good at school. He had come to this university purely by chance. Mostly because both Liyana and Ahmed were there. He was only studying computer engineering and cybersecurity because they were.

What he wanted to study was botany, but his father scoffed at the idea. Adana could recall his exact words and repeat them verbatim if asked to do so. Even now, the words were running around in his head.

"Botany! What the heck is that even supposed to be!" he had shouted. "You'll never get a job anywhere if you study botany! Do you want to work in the garden shop down the street? If you wanted that, why did you have me pay thousands and thousands of rupees to send you to all of these schools and academies through all these years if you want to go and become nothing better than a *Mali*!"

His father had been unsatisfied that this was something that he loved and what he could see himself doing for years and years to come without getting bored, or growing tired of it. It brought him so much joy to watch seeds turn into plants, flowers, and then trees.

Compared to that, the world of engineering and computers was stark and empty; the thought of having to work a nine-to-five job, stuck in an office all day, all the time, made him feel like he was going to go mad.

He knew he wasn't the only person at that university that felt that way. There were so many students studying many different fields who were doing it because their parents had asked. It wasn't their dream, not there calling, it wasn't their choice; it was just something that they were told to do. And like obedient sheep, they did it.

Adana wondered how many of them were like him merely going through the motions of getting up, going to class, and coming home, never feeling engaged, making any kind of contribution, or finding their place because it wasn't something that they love.

On the other hand, he was lucky to have friends like Ahmed and Liyana; without them, attending the university would have been pure hell. *Speaking of friends, where are they?* Adana turned around to look; they were still arguing about something. He wanted to laugh but just watched.

Adana watched as his friends stood side by side, arguing about something. With a sign, he kept walking. They would catch up. Sometimes he wished that they would just tell each other how they felt so that he could finally stop having to listen to the both of them go on and on about how they thought about the other.

If he thought it would help them, he would tell the truth for them, but the fact of the matter was until one, or both of them grew confident enough to tell the other how they felt, it would never work because, as usual, Adana was stuck in the middle.

He just wanted some food so he could sort out what needed to be completed for the class assignment.

"Yo! Liyana's buying food," Ahmed stated as he came up next to him and threw his arm across his shoulder. He pulled his head toward him. "So, remember to get a lot, she's gonna foot the bill." He laughed as Liyana took a mock swing toward him.

They made their way toward the university cafeteria, Adana and Ahmed trying to pull the other under their arm as Liyana watched their antics into the building. Life was good when you were around people you cared about every day.

***

Hakim Omar was annoyed. He had been told that he would be able to find the man he needed to get this job done; instead, he encountered one failure after another. This job was going to be the death of him. How hard could it possibly be to hack into a single account of a single man? Why were none of the people he hired able to do it?

The frustration got to him. He needed to get this

job over with soon or go mad from the annoyances he faced during this trying time. There was no other way around this; he simply had to find the right person and then force them into working for him through some kind of nefarious means.

He knew the perfect picking ground for young potential hackers. He would begin his search today; it shouldn't take him exceedingly long to find the right candidate.

Chapter Two

Ahmed received a call from his mother. As usual, she seemed to want to vent about his father. They had been separated for three years, but at every opportunity, she called him to talk about her husband. It bothered him, not because he didn't understand his mother; it was he wanted her to move on from his father. He loved both his parents, but his father was not the best specimen of a loving husband.

As far back as he could remember, Ahmed had seen his father neglect his mother continually. In the brief instances, he acknowledged her presence; it would be to admonish her or to point out some perceived fault. To put it bluntly, his dad was an asshole.

Ahmed didn't want to be like him. When he married, he wanted to treat his wife better, not because she had every right to be treated with respect, but he wanted to set a positive example for his children if he had any.

As he made his way toward the door, he took a moment to gather his bearings.

"*Ammi!* I'm at the door, where are you? Did you make anything for lunch? I'm starving," Ahmed said as he walked into the house. He was starving but having something in his mouth would give him the bonus of not having to respond to her attempts to probe him for information about his father.

"Ahmed! You came to see me! Oh, how lovely!" His mum, with a bright smile on her face, stood at the top of the stairs looking at him. He resisted the urge to roll his eyes at her surprise. He wasn't dropping in; she had called him just hours earlier, complaining that he didn't visit enough. Of course, she would conveniently forget that they had had dinner together only two days ago. She tended to have a selective memory when it suited her.

Hira Abbas was forty-three years old, but the years had been kind to her. She could easily pass for someone younger. As she glided down the stairs, Ahmed felt a twinge of pity for his mother. She was a lovely woman; she was what one could call classically pretty, with soft but well-defined features, fair skin, and big eyes, which all seemed to be desirable traits among women, at least to his knowledge. It wouldn't be too hard for his mother to meet someone and start a life with them.

"You wanted something to eat, right?" She asked as she reached the last step. She wove her arm through his, linking them together and walked in the direction of the dining room.

"I had *keema mutter* and some *saag paneer* prepared, such a happy coincidence, don't you think? I know you love them. See, I was thinking of you all day. Did you hear about…" She continued to talk, and Ahmed tuned her out as he thought about the food.

He wasn't trying to be rude, and to be honest, his mother would talk to the lamp if she thought it would respond with the occasional hum and haw of acknowledgment. All he could think about was the food. Since his brief meal with Liyana and Adnan in the university cafeteria, he hadn't eaten all day.

Ahmed prepared himself to have to listen to all the things that his mother would complain about. He just hoped the food would taste good. As long as he could eat, he would be fine. As he sat down with her, he took a moment to consider what he could do to help her. She needed to divorce his father.

It was the only solution at this point. Separation still gave his father far too many rights and privileges when it came to his mother. Ahmed needed to figure out a better way for his mother. She could not continue to stay trapped like this, slowly being driven to madness by the pressures and expectations that his father put continuously on her or even though their marriage was nothing but a public facade and a sham.

"Mom? Have you ever considered getting a divorce from dad? I mean, do you think it would be better if you just stopped seeing him? I don't think that being separated is working for both of you. I hate that it makes you so upset all the time. I hate that you have to put on a show whenever he needs to go out into the public, show off to his friends, or if he wants his colleagues to come by for a meal."

His mom sighed.

"Do you realise how much I love you? I love that you

want to protect me from this, but the truth is, I need your father as much as he needs me. We have this sort of symbiotic relationship at this point. A rather toxic one perhaps, less symbiotic, and more parasitic, but we fulfil the social and financial requirements for each other." She took a long deep breath. "It might sound cold to most people, but we've always had this kind of marriage despite how much I like to complain to you about it. I don't complain because I'm still in love with your father. I do it because, if I'm honest, well, it's pure spite." She casually took a bite of her food, pretending that nothing happened.

Ahmed slowly swallowed his food, and with a confused shake of his head, continued to eat.

***

Liyana and Adnan worked on his assignment. He needed help with coming up with a script for his new AI model. It was a rather rudimentary creation, but it was the best that he could do. Adana had never really been good at these sorts of things, and Liyana understood that.

She knew that he had only joined this university because his parents had pressured him into it, and she always tried to listen to him when he had a hard time coping with classes and managing the stress of having to deal with his father daily.

"Do you know, if maybe he'll let you do a masters in something other than tech? I know you said you've talked to him about this before, but have you tried maybe to convince your mom to help you? I get that she doesn't like getting involved between the two of you to avoid fighting with him. And I can appreciate that, but you're her son!" Liyana was trying to be helpful, but he knew his parents all too well.

His mother would never step in. Both of them shared a somewhat antiquated opinion on gender roles. His father was of the view - the wrong belief, in Adana's opinion, that women were the lesser gender. This made it so that anything that his mother said was disregarded, dismissed, or simply ignored. His father didn't believe that she had anything useful to say.

The man barely even tolerated his relationship with Liyana. He couldn't understand how Adana and Liyana could be friends.

"Trust me, I've tried. I've tried so many times at this point, but I feel like if I push one more time, he might decide to cut me off and throw me out." Adana adjusted his grip on his pencil. He drew a botanical sketch as Liyana watched. "I've pushed this issue too far already. I just need to graduate first. Once I get a job somewhere, maybe I can study part time. It would take me years, but I could still do something in botany." He filled in the sketch a bit more. "I can't let him control my life forever, I love him despite his faults, I don't want to; I don't want to resent him ten years down the line because he didn't let me do something. I'd rather make him happy now so I can have peace of mind later."

Liyana thought Adana was being ridiculous, as usual, but she kept her opinion to herself. It wouldn't help him at all if she told him that.

"I hope it does work out, but you know if he *does* kick you out, you know my mom would love to have you around. She keeps saying she misses hearing the sound of a guy in the house, I don't know how that's possible, considering that she has been a widow for more than twelve years, and I don't have a brother."

"Thank you," Adana added with a roll of his eyes; he knew she was just humouring him, but it was still nice to see that she cared.

They were sitting in Liyana's room as she helped him with the algorithm while he drew. He had already done most of the work; it just needed a bit of refining, and Liyana was better at that than both him and Ahmed.

***

Ten Months Earlier

Sub-Inspector Lal Zaman was a rather large man with an equally massive moustache. His wife often told him that his moustache resembled that of a hotel doorman. She often joked that he could simply dress up in the red uniform and put on their turban, and no one would notice that there had been any change.

The sub-inspector was by all accounts an imposing man. He was at six feet four, a relative giant amongst his colleagues. With his dark skin and cat-like green eyes, Lal Zaman was what you could call intimidating.

No one knew this better than the criminals who he apprehended. Upon seeing Lal Zaman approach, they always scattered like rats because a man of his size could only be one of two things, a loan shark's henchman coming to collect money or a policeman. Neither option was appealing to anyone who had debts or was on the run from the law.

Lal made his way across the precinct to his superior's office. He had been called in after being told that he was being reassigned to a new department. As far as he knew, there were no new openings for any of sub-inspector post in any of the department in the city.

That could only mean that he was being transferred to another city. He couldn't have that his whole life here. His wife would hate to move, especially after the fact that he had forced her to come to live here instead of up north because he'd wanted to become a policeman.

His family had disowned him for wanting to become a law enforcement officer. Mariam, his wife, had made the difficult choice of coming with him instead of remaining with the tribe where she would have been fine without him.

Lal didn't know what he was going to say to her if he was told today that he had to move to a different city. God alone knew where that would be. It was already too hot here, for someone who had grown up in the northern mountains.

With the snow and the long winters, he couldn't imagine what would happen if he had to live in one of the cities like Multan or Karachi, where the weather was even hotter.

With a knock, he entered his superior's office. "Sir! Sub-inspector Lal Zaman reporting for duty! Sir!" With a salute, he stood by the door, waiting to be acknowledged.

"Oh! It's you. Come, come, sit down. I have something

important to tell you," His CO's informal
response threw him off. He took a seat that was in front
of his desk.

"Yes sir," He said before awkwardly lowering himself
into the chair.

"Don't look so worried; it's all good news. You're
about to be promoted to Inspector."

Lal was beyond surprised; he couldn't understand how
this was possible. He hadn't done anything in the
recent months to warrant this unexpected promotion.
He looked back and tried to see if there was anything
in memory that could be the cause of this promotion.

He couldn't think of a single thing that happened in
the last few months, in fact, even the previous year;
that could have prompted a significant change like
this. He was well aware that the police department
was extremely corrupt. Promotions like this often
went to officers who had done something for
someone higher up, and for the life of him, he
couldn't remember anything significant like that.

"Sir, if I may ask, what led to this promotion, sir?" he
asked hesitantly not quite believing what was
happening. "I'm not sure if this is the right move. I don't
think I've done anything to merit a promotion like this."

Lal watched as his superior's face turned rather sheepish. He couldn't understand why the man was feeling embarrassed. There wasn't anything that had happened involving hid superior that could be construed as embarrassing, considering Lal didn't work on the kind of cases that might lead to someone like his superior having cause to be embarrassed.

"Well, you see, the Commissioner has decided that we need a new task force because there has been a rise in a certain type of crime. I was asked who some of my best officers were, and I gave your name on that list. But truth be told, do you want a reason you seem to have been picked?" The embarrassment was back. "It is because you were the only candidate. I had listed that I hadn't completed any form of higher education." His superior was practically squirming in his seat as he informed Lal of what was happening.

It slowly dawned on him the commissioner didn't want this task force to do well. Clearly, some politicians were putting pressure on him to create this task force in hopes of furthering whatever agenda they had. For whatever reason, the commissioner had decided to indulge them by giving in and creating this task force.

However, he was wasn't trying extremely hard to find people that could make any difference. He felt a twinge of anger at the fact that he was being used. He was on the police force; he was not a pawn in a political chess game, and unlike many of his colleagues, he didn't appreciate this kind of treatment, despite the promotion.

"So, you're telling me that the Police Commissioner has decided to put me in charge of a task force because I'm under-qualified to run it? Am I saying that correctly? Do I have it right?"

"Well, you see Lal; the thing is that I don't know what to say. I'm embarrassed, and I feel ashamed that I work under a man who is capable of doing this. But the truth of the matter is that neither one of us has a choice in this matter."

"I have no choice. I have to give this to someone, and that someone is you. Get read and pack your things. I'll give you some men to start off with from this precinct, and in the next few weeks, officers from other precincts will begin arriving."

Lal walked out of his office, not sure about what had just happened, feeling somewhat dejected about the whole thing. He robotically gathered the things from his desk and if any of his colleagues asked him any questions, he did not remember

answering them, much less what the questions.
This was a sign that significant changes were
coming. The only questions were what kind of
changes they would be and would bode well for
him? He was disappointed that his life was guiding
him down a rather unlikely path. Lal Zaman
sincerely hoped that whatever the future would
hold for him, it was nothing too disastrous.
Wanting to live a quiet, uneventful life with
nothing much remarkable in it wasn't a lot to ask
for in Lal's opinion. However, it seemed that fate
had something far more intriguing planned for
him.

As Lal walked toward his desk for what would be the
last time for a long while, he pulled out his chair and
plopped down with a rather loud sigh. Big changes
were indeed coming, and while he hoped they would
bode well for him, he sincerely doubted that would be
the case. There were many things that Lal was willing
to compromise on when it came to his new office;
however, there was one thing that he was not ready
to compromise on a single bit -- tea. Speaking of tea,
he was going to walk over and make a cup for himself;
tea was good for all situations, especially stressful
ones like this.

Chapter Three

"I need to do this, Adnan!" Ahmed exclaimed as he paced the room. "I need to tell her how I feel!" Adnan scoffs as he listens to Ahmed, remembering all the other times he had said this and chickened out.

"Come on, man! You always say this and then back down," Adnan took a puff of his cigarette, "Then every week or so, we are right back here, and you talk about how last time was different and that you will *actually* do it this time. You gotta man up! Gotta tell her how you feel once and for all before some guy with real balls does it first." At his last comment, Ahmed threw his friend an angry glare, but Adana shrugged it off;

the truth hurt, but someone had to say it.

Ahmed looked at his friend, a frown on his face; he knew he was right, and he knew that he has wanted to confess his feelings to Liyana for years now. They had been friends ever since he could remember, but it was when he was twelve that he realized that he had begun to like her as more than a friend.

The problem was that Ahmed was afraid to talk about his feelings with her as he deeply feared she would reject his confession and, in doing so, permanently damage their relationship. He wasn't sure when he had come to this conclusion, but he was reasonably certain that Liyana had strong feelings for him.

However, what he didn't know was what those strong feelings were. He could never be sure until he actually went out of his way to ask her. And to be perfectly honest, that was not happening.

"Adana, I don't wanna lose her." He said almost painfully. Ahmed was so unsure of himself that at times it was almost embarrassing.

"Trust me, bro, telling her how you feel is the best solution for this. I know this sounds insane, but trust me." He implored, "Once you tell her how you feel, it will make things better, and I just know, in my gut, that things will work out between the two of you." Adana was so sure of himself that for a moment, Ahmed believed everything that he said.

"Okay, I've decided I'm telling you everything, I'm going to do it this weekend after the freshers party. She will be in a good mood. And maybe I get her alone, probably for a bit, and we can talk about this." He was convinced now was the right time to do this. He had been putting this off for so long, but he believed that if he waited around any longer, without actually saying anything, it wouldn't be long before Liyana met another guy. A guy who would sweep her off her feet, and he would be brave enough actually to say how he felt. It would be too late then.

"I'm proud of you. I know you can do this. Just trust yourself." Adana put his hand on top of Ahmed's shoulder, patting it almost reassuringly. "Really, you can do it, and once you do this, you will realize how much happier you are having done it." With another squeeze of Ahmed's shoulder, Adana started to shift around. "Now, I need to head home."

"Is everything alright?" Ahmed looked over at his friend, hoping that everything was okay. He was well aware of how strained Adana's relationship was with his father, and how stressed out he always was about it.

"Yeah, yeah! It's all good. Don't worry?" Adana reassured him there was no point going into the finer details of what was going on. It wouldn't help Ahmed to understand the situation any better, and it would honestly just embarrass Adana to talk about it.

"Okay, you're sure?" He asked again.

"Bro, it's all good." He said as he stood up, gathering his things as he moved around the terrace. He exited the balcony and walked into Ahmed's room. He sprayed himself with some deodorant from Ahmed's dresser, hopefully it would lead to a decent enough job to cover up the smell of the cigarette smoke that was lingering on his clothes. He scanned the room to see if he forgot anything. Not that it mattered if he did, Ahmed would just bring it to the shared house they lived in.

During the week, when they had classes, the boys lived at the house they shared rent. On every other one of the weekends; however, their parents had them come and stay with them. Adana knew it wasn't because they missed them or anything; it was purely so they could keep an eye on them at least that was the motivation his father had. Speaking of his father, he gave his clothes another cursory sniff; the spell of Tabaco was faint. By the time he got home, it would have dissipated.

He didn't need the added stress of arguing with his father about his smoking, on top of whatever it was that his father wanted to discuss with him today.

***

Adana's parents lived in an average-sized house in Defense. They were not the wealthiest people amongst their acquaintances, but they were comfortable. As Adana made his way toward the house, his stomach filled with dread. He felt like he had swallowed a block of led, and it was pressing into his gut.

He and his father did not have the best relationship growing up. Like his antiquated views on gender roles, Adana's father had a strange notion of what relationships between parents and children should be like.

He did not believe that parents and their children should have the kind of relationship where frankness and informality were abundant. He thought that one should respect their parent beyond any other person, and that formality and distance should always be maintained between the two.

He wasn't one to dispense away with such ideas even though he was surrounded by people who showed open affection to their children, joked with them, and spoke to them informally. None of these things could prompt Ali Abdullah to change his stance on anything.

Ali was a firm believer in holding with tradition. Even when he could see that these traditions were in all effect strangling and killing off any relationships he had, most importantly, it had damaged his relationship with his son forever. Ali's stubbornness and refusal to budge on issues that were most assuredly pushing his son further and further away from him as time went on, was proof that the man was unmovable.

As Adana approached his home, he noticed that unlike all the other times, his father had been angry at him, waiting at the porch for him to enter so that he could scold him, his father was not there. Hopefully, this was a sign that whatever was coming was not something to fear, but he just could not push that feeling away.

With his dread continuing to grow, Adana walked into his house, hoping that whatever fate awaited him, it was not too bad.

***

Liyana stretched out on her yoga matt and took a

long deep breath. She moved into the downward dog position, before holding a plank for thirty seconds. The soft tantric music playing in the background was accompanied by the soft and sublet sounds of chirping birds and the bubbling of a brook.

The soundtrack continued to play as Liyana moved from one pose to the next, keeping her breathing steady, and trying to relax. It was hard to relax. Her mind was running at a hundred miles a minute, as she tried not to think about today.

She could not get Ahmed out if her mind. When Adana had been over at her house today, she had barely resisted the urge to confront him. She wanted him to tell her if he thought that Ahmed felt the same way about her as she did him.

In the last two years, Liyana's feelings for one of her best friends had changed drastically; she was no longer just thought of him as just a friend. He was more than that. Way more than that, he was someone that she was profoundly and probably irreversibly in love with.

She wasn't sure where it started, or even when. Much less how or why. All she knew was that with every fibre of her being, she was in love with

Ahmed.

It terrified her.

Not because he wasn't a good person, or because there was anything wrong with him. She was terrified because she didn't know if he felt the same way; she was afraid that if she told him how she felt, and he didn't feel the same way, it would damage their friendship forever.

There was no going back from confessions like that. Liyana had seen it time and time again with friends, girls, or guys who had confessed about their feelings only to find that they were rejected, and in doing so, had lost the friendship of the person they confessed to.

It was extremely strenuous on any relationship when it was imbalanced. The responsibility of knowing that your friend felt a certain way about you and that you didn't reciprocate those feelings meant that this relationship was now imbalanced. With the equilibrium disturbed, there was no going back.

At times Liyana felt like she was like a computer infected with a virus or malware that she had no firewalls against and no system to fight back. Although truthfully, she did not want to fight back. She didn't regret being in love with her best friend. She had no regrets except for the fact that she hadn't told him how she felt.

Liyana had concluded that it was high time that she bucked up, put on her big girl boots, and told him how she felt. She had discussed this with her mother quite recently.

As she moved from one yoga pose to another, she thought back to the day she had told her mother how she felt about her best friend.

Her mom, Professor Hinna Azan, was the kind of mother who one could always count on to be supportive. She was always there to listen. Liyana did not doubt that her mother would always be on her side, no matter what she did, what she said, and regardless of any mistakes she made.

***

One Week Earlier
Liyana was sitting at the table with her mother, the two of them were enjoying a nice Italian dinner together. Her mother had decided to cook today. Hinna was an excellent cook. Liyana was always envious of her mother's ability to throw together simple ingredients and come out with a dish that

tasted and looked amazing.

Liyana looked at her mother, the two of them bore a strong resemblance to one another. Whenever and wherever they were together, it didn't take people long to realise that they were mother and daughter. They shared the same light chocolate brown hair, creamy light mocha skin, and heart-shaped face. The truly distinguishing feature between the two of them was their eye colour. Where Hinna had lovely cloud grey eyes, Liyana had gotten her eyes from her father; they were a dark deep warm hazel. Liyana Was also the shorter of the two, at five-foot-four, while her mother stood at five-foot-eight barefoot, she was rather tall for a woman in their country.

"Mom, I have something... I wanted to there's something that I want to tell you about... I mean to you... I mean that I have something I want to talk to you about or more specifically get your opinion on." Liyana started hesitantly. She wasn't sure why she was so worried about this; it wasn't as if her mother would suddenly reject her or disown her for having these thoughts.

Her mother had always been incredibly supportive of all the things that Liyana decided to do, even though she didn't always approve of her decisions, she never held her back from making her own mistakes. However, at this moment, what she really needed was not her mother's support but rather her opinion.

"The truth of the matter is... well what I mean is... I... I... I'm in love." She blurted out.

She looked at her mother, waiting to see her reaction. Her mother's face remained quite neutral. She had not so much as had a micro expression change since Liyana made her confession two seconds ago.

Hinna continued to chew her food slowly. With a slow, deliberate swallow, she licked her lips clean clearing the pasta sauce, bit her lip between her canines, before smiling. Her grey eyes were lighting up as if the sun peeked through around rain clouds.

"Sweetheart! that's wonderful." She exclaimed with a genuinely happy smile on her face. "Do I know who the lucky boy is?" she asked, with genuine curiosity.

Her reaction was positive, for now, which reassured Liyana. However, she wasn't sure how her mother would respond when she found out who the object of her feelings was. To be honest, despite feeling this way for almost two years now, Liyana herself was unsure about *why* she felt that way.

"Well, you see, the person I'm in love with... well, it's.... it's Ahmed?" She stuttered out ending her statement with a question. Almost as if she wanted her mother's approval on her choice or rather the person that had claimed her affections.

"Oh, Liyana, that's wonderful! He's such a lovely boy. I couldn't have picked someone better if I tried!" Her mother was not lying; Liyana knew exactly what it looked like when she was, because her mother was a lousy liar, and right now, she had her mother's full support.

She got up from her seat at the table and went over and hugged her mother hard. She genuinely needed this reassurance; without it, she wasn't sure she would have had the courage to confess to Ahmed finally. The only other person who knew how she felt was Adana and to be perfectly honest he was hardly the most objective person in this situation, considering that he was best friends with both people involved in the situation.

"You don't know how happy it makes me to hear that you approve, I was so worried that you would be angry."

"Oh, no dear, why would you think that? I'm always

happy for you. The only thing that I want from you is to be happy in life. I don't need you to have a job that makes millions or cure the world of cancer or anything ridiculous like that. Like most parents, the only thing I want from you is your happiness, and to be honest, I have come to realise that Ahmed makes you happy." She squeezed her daughter back, tightening her arms around her. Hinn was happy for her child.

"I was a bit worried about how you would react to what I told you, I know that it was a silly worry, but it was still there. You're always so accepting of everything that I do. Sometimes it's like waiting for the other shoe to drop. I worry that one day do or say something that'll disappoint you so much I won't even realise that crossed the line because you've always kept it so blurry," Liyana said with a whisper.

"Trust me, you don't have to worry about that. There will never be a time that you could do anything that could hurt me or disappoint me enough not to be able to forgive you," she said. She gave Liyana another hug and kissed the top of her head as she stroked her hair. Hinna Azan loved her only child with every fibre of every cell of her person. She wanted to be supportive of the fact that her daughter had found somebody that she could share such deep feelings for. She just hoped that Ahmed felt the same way about her that she did him.

When Liyana confessed her feelings, and she undoubtedly would, considering that she was telling her mother how she felt. Hinna hoped that she was not rejected. There was nothing worse than seeing your child in pain, knowing the cause, and be completely powerless to help them.

They held each other, both for reassurance and for the sake of simply being helped by another person. Liyana felt more loved at that moment than she ever had. Her mother had always been an affectionate parent, always trying to fill the hole left behind by the death of her father.

Her mother's family continuously tried to push for her to remarry, and over the years, there had been few men that would have made her genuinely happy. Still, he never did get remarried, and it wasn't because there were no options or that she didn't want to. She didn't because of Liyana. She didn't trust a stranger could raise her daughter with the same love and affection that she could. She did not want to risk her daughter's unhappiness just so that she could have her own.

Liyana felt a surge of love for her mother. This had given her that final boost she needed. It was now the time to tell Ahmed how she felt. She would do it soon before this month was out. If she did not do it now, then there was no point in torturing her-self further on this matter.

Chapter Four

The Punjab state prison outside of Lahore was a massive structure. It had been around since before the time of the British occupation and had served as a military garrison, until at some point during its long history, it had been modified to a prison. The looming granite and cement walls were the newest part of the prison, having been extended and thickened in the last decade or so. Most of the rest of the prison was at least seventy years old. It was one of the largest prisons in the country but also one of the worst.

Not only in its treatment of prisoners, with the frequent complaints of abuse, neglect, and starvation, but also because it seemed to house some of the worst criminals in the country in its highest security north-western wing. Hakim had never been unfortunate enough to have to stay at the prison, but he had heard enough second-hand accounts to know that ending up behind those doors in the maximum-security wing was almost always a death sentence for first and second-time prisoners. The guards were not much help in protecting prisons or preventing and policing prisoner on prisoner violence.

Today Hakim Omar was there to pick up a former 'guest' of this institution. He had known this man for many years, and he was a hardened criminal; however, he seemed to have the world's greatest luck at times. Hakim could swear that it was only because he had made some bargain with a *jinn*[6] and was cashing in on that luck.

He could not understand how a convicted criminal like Qadir Ramez, with the kind of record that he had kept managing to get out on parole. This had to be the fourth time he had managed to slip away without having to serve his full sentence. The man was a rather slippery snake.

"Oyy! So, you finally showed your ugly face!" Qadir roared as he stepped out of the prison gates.

Hakim pushed off the side of his car where he had been leaning up as he waited, with the momentum of the push still working he walked rapidly toward Qadir. They had known each other for years now, and they would often do jobs together.

Qadir was found of Hakim, as fond as one criminal can be for another. However, there was something about Hakim that even made Qadir's skin crawl. It was that uncomfortable knowledge that something about Hakim was not quite right. Qadir was a hardened criminal, and at thirty-one he was hardly a young man. It took more than a dirty look from someone to unnerve him. Hakim could do it by just being in the room.

The first time Qadir had met Hakim, it was on a bad night. Hakim had just lost a pool match to a young man in the Pool Hall. The boy had pretended to suck at pool and had conned Hakim into betting a large amount of money. Hakim was an enthusiastic gambler. He didn't give up easily, but he wasn't the kind of person who took losing well. In fact, he took it very badly.

Qadir was a firsthand witness to the brutally merciless way Hakim could react in a situation. The boy, who even after all these years Hakim could not remember the name of, he could recall what happened in excruciating detail.

***

Six Years Ago

The Pool Hall, which was in the basement of a tech phone shop, was a popular hangout for a rather unsavory crowd. You could find all sorts here from hardened lifetime criminals, to the unaccepted people that lingered on the fringe of polite society. The ceiling was low, it was barely seven feet, and the walls had been white at some point, but now they were a dull brown. It was hard to tell what all the stains on the walls were.

Some splatters near the pool table in the back looked suspiciously like dried blood. The rest of the stains were anyone's guess. However, he doubted anyone wanted to try to think too hard about the origins of those stains.

There was a bar in the back; the alcohol was hidden behind strategically placed compartments in the unlikely event that the police decided to perform a raid, looking for alcohol. The bar was a solid slab of dark wood and easily the only clean piece of furniture in the room. The seating in the bar was minimal and was almost always claimed by someone or the other.

No one was stupid enough to sit on one of the sofas or chairs. All of them had owners; all of them were men that nobody wanted to run into in a dark alley or a shadowy road.

Most of the regulars in the pool hall were parolees or ex-convicts. There was the occasional young buck who wandered in on a whim. A chance to walk on the dark side, but more often, they took a look around, saw the general hostility in the air, and walked right back out unmolested, minus the occasional missing wallet.

However, this time something was different. The newcomer had decided to play against Hakim completely unaware of the decision that he had made and the consequences of that decision. The game started simple. Hakim took a shot, and it landed in the pocket. The boy would try, and he would fail, Hakim would go again.

This continued for two games, and it seemed like the newcomer was about to lose all his money, when he decided to challenge Hakim to a winner takes all game.

"You don't think I could win, do you?" The boy said.

Hakim laughed, shook his head as if the laughter was overwhelming him.

"Kid! You have no chance; you can't beat me! Have you seen the way you've been playing today? It's gonna take a miracle for you to win."

"Miracle? Huh? Well, you're gonna make a miracle if you're up for it?" The boys laughed arrogantly.

Hakim lined up the balls, setting the triangle at the center. He decided to let the boy break first.

"You're sure old man? I think I know how to play this game; looks like I might win this time."
Hakim just nodded. "Go on, take your best shot, but remember winner takes all." He emphasized with a thump of his pool cue.

The boy took a stance behind the white ball, took aim, and broke. The ball he hit went forward with such force that it scattered all the balls in various directions and pocketed two. He called solids and began pocketing each ball one after another in quick succession.

Hakim was left standing embarrassed shown up by this young boy.

Qadir didn't know him at all back then, and he wasn't sure at first how he would react to the embarrassment.

Qadir, like the others, stood watching as the game

progressed, and it became very apparent Hakim had just been hustled. No one was quite sure what to do; this was the first time something like this had happened, and especially to someone like Hakim, who, by all counts, was one of the best pool players that came to this hall.

It wasn't unheard of for newbies to come around and beat old players, but the fact that this happened to Hakim with everyone watching made them all apprehensive. All of them knew what Hakim was like.

Qadir had never seen Hakim get mad before as he didn't know him that well. They had only run into each other at the occasional night at the pool hall and, at times, working a job that required a hacker and a car thief to be present at the same time, which in itself was a rarity. So, Qadir could say he didn't know Hakim that well. However, from their brief interactions, he at least thought he was a stable person.

That day he witnessed some of the worst violence he had ever seen, not because it was particularly grotesque, but because it happened almost without provocation and was instantaneous.

As the young man stood laughing, proclaiming his victory for all to see, Hakim stood silent slowly breathing in and out as if he was trying to control his anger. It wasn't working because with every breath, his breathing became more and more accelerated, and he seemed to become more and more agitated instead of calmer.

In the blink of an eye, and honestly, Qadir didn't even notice when it happened, but Hakim had the boy pinned on the pool table.

He brought his mouth close to the boy's ear and whispered something. No one ever dared to ask what Hakim had said, but whatever he said turned the boy pale. His face drained of color, going pale and ghostly as he realized what had just happened.

He was now at Hakim's mercy, in a place where there was no mercy. Whatever promise of violence Hakim made to the boy in that terrifying quiet whisper in his ear, no doubt that Hakim held up his end of the bargain.

Slowly, with almost loving caress, Hakim ran his fingers through the boy's hair, as he used his other hand to bend his arm behind his back and hold him against the pool table. "Do you know what happens to boys who pretend their men? Do you know what I do to boys who pretend they're men?" He said loud enough that everyone in the pool hall heard him. The whole place had gone silent as they watched him steadily lose to the boy, almost as if in anticipation of what was to follow.

The gentle caressing hand in the boy's hair turned into a claw that gripped and pulled. It pulled his head back almost until the boy was standing with his back arched as Hakim held his hand behind his back. With a sickening crunch, Hakim brought his face down onto the pool table. There was a spurt of blood as his nose broke on impact, and the scream followed seconds later -- loud, agonizing, and full of surprise.

Hakim pulled his hair back again, bringing his face down for a second time. Only this time, his teeth hit the edge of the table, and the scream was muffled covered by the gurgles of blood coming from his mouth and nose.

No one stepped forward to stop him. No one said anything. They watched, silent, somber, and just a little bit terrified as Hakim slammed the boy's face over and over and over again into the pool table until it was nothing but a gory bleeding lump, where the boy's face had once been.

Almost, as if he were unaware of the stir he had caused, Hakim filtered through the boy's pockets removing his earnings, placed them in his pocket, and with a final kick toward the boy's face walked away. "Now you know what I do to boys who pretend to be men."

Qadir, in all his years, had never seen such unprecedented violence. The reaction was so overblown for what had happened you couldn't quite wrap your head around it. Most of the people left in the pool hall were all too afraid to go near the boy and too afraid that Hakim would return and see them helping the boy and take his wrath out on them.

Just like all the others, Qadir walked away as well, but not before he took one final look at the boy lying on the floor. He wasn't moving; he wasn't making a sound, Qadir was doubtful if he was even alive.

Scared and a little bit disgusted, Qadir walked away, trying to put off this feeling of foreshadowing as he saw Hakim cross the road and not see him as he walked onward in whatever direction he was going. Hakim barely remembered what had happened that night, and he didn't care. Qadir never quite forgot that moment and he never would.

***

Now, he stood be before him years later, and Qadir was filled with apprehension. He couldn't quite understand why he felt that way, but he did.

"Now that you have left the custody of our lovely state, what do you want to do?" Hakim asked Qadir as they walked toward Hakim's car.

Qadir took a moment to just breathe in the air. He knew it was hardly logical, but the air inside the prison had always felt like it was going to choke him.

It was the same air, the prison was hardly twenty feet away from him, but the difference felt astronomical. If he ever got caught again, Qadir did not think he would be able to survive another trip in the prison. He would rather spend the rest of his life running from the law, than to spend even one more day inside another prison.

"Somewhere with food, and then let's find someone to keep me company. Fifteen months is too long without seeing a beautiful woman." Qadir laughed as they got into Hakim's car. When he was seated in the passenger seat, he took a second to look at himself in the rearview mirror. His scar had healed relatively well. He had been attacked with a shive by an unstable inmate only a few days after arriving at the prison. He ran his finger over his scarred cheek. The cut started out just below his left eye, making a path toward his ear before curving sharply toward his mouth. It had ended just above his jawbone.

At least it was his left side, Qadir thought to himself. He believed that his profile from the right was much better anyway.

"Oh, I know just the place where you can meet, some very pretty girls!" Hakim laughed as they drove off. "Even better, I have managed to find a guy I need for a job, we can meet him there, and you can find yourself some company."

"And where exactly is there?" Qadir asked.

"A freshman party at the Tech Uni, you know the one, it where we recruited that Faiza boy for the Tariq job," Hakim explained.

"Aah, I remember him. Didn't he end up getting shot or something?" Qadir glanced over at Hakim as he asked him the question. The man driving the car had not changed much since they had first met.

He was older now, of course, and the last eight years or so had left their marks, be he had not changed in the sense that his personality was exactly the same. He was still prone to spontaneous bursts of explosive anger. He would almost blackout and commit horrible acts of violence, only to come back to himself, and only have a vague recollection of the violence that he had committed.

The rage Qadir could understand. Hakim was a boy who grow up rough on the streets and not be hardened by the difficulties of life. What he did worry about was the fact that he never seemed to feel any remorse for his actions.

He would commit acts of violence and look back on them with the same amount of regard one would have for stepping on an ant, no guilt, and certainly no repentance.

"Sounds good, but you mind grabbing some food first. I was tired of all the fucking *dal*[7] they gave us," Qadir chuckled.

"Of course, let's go get you some real food," Hakim said with a strange smile, which made Qadir shudder as they drove off, leaving the prison gates behind them.

***

Hakim had brought Qadir to a party after grabbing something to eat. The two of them were quite obviously out of place among all of these college students. Not only were they clearly so much older than all the people here, they were also obviously not of the same status.

The country had a class system that was rather obvious and obscured at the same time, which is exactly what Hakim's plan for tonight seemed like.

Hakim had said they were here to meet someone that he wanted to recruit for the job. Qadir was unsure of how they were going about doing that by arranging for a bunch or somewhat random chance incidences to occur. Unfortunately, he was not the one in charge, and as far as anyone was concerned, his thoughts did not matter one bit.

With a loud sigh, Qadir wove his way through the throng of bodies so that he could reach the spot that Hakim had told him to wait at and instigate the events that would allow for Hakim and his target for the night to meet, by what would seem like random chance.

Chapter Five

Ahmed wanted to celebrate. He had completed his third successful account hacking. It had started out as a theoretical exercise in his second-year cybersecurity class about firewalls and how various hacking software's get around them.

Their professor had them develop a type of malware that would bypass firewalls and, in doing so, record keystrokes, and so on. Ahmed had become over-enthusiastic about it, and instead of just developing a theoretical form of this malware, he had come up with the actual malware.

It was a genius piece of cyber tech, in his opinion. He

had designed a pop up add style cover that when you dismiss it, instead of disappearing, it becomes merely invisible. As you continue to browse and use your internet or even your phone, it uses a rather simplistic AI algorithm to analyses and record your data. It simultaneously records your keystrokes so that it can record all your data on a third-party app, and then it can analyse it so that it may find patterns and, in doing so, assesses what your passwords.

On a lark, Ahmed had decided to try to see if it could be used in a practical setting. He had not intended to take if further than just trying it out and then erasing the personal data he collected. At least that was what he told himself.

He had decided to get some publicly available emails of random people from his professors to local businesses and some politicians. He had then composed an inconspicuous email with the malware embedded and sent it out. The results had been impressive, and he had learned some startling things about the people that the emails went to. Some of them had been plain weird, others disgusting, and some extremely funny.

He had learned that the assistant professor for one of his coding modules, a one Sarah Tariq, was part of a

Facebook group where the participants actively pretended to be ants in a colony. They had a Queen who they always referred to as 'The Queen' in caps, and they all referred to themselves in binary numbers and actively participated in this roleplay without coming out of character. It was one of the most bizarre things Ahmed had ever seen, but at the same time oddly endearingly funny.

However, it was by no means the only strange thing he had found. He discovered that one of the Junior MP's in the city had a rather strong fetish for feet. He had hundreds upon hundreds of pictures of feet saved on his hard drives and his computer. That one was just plain weird. For the life of him, Ahmed could not understand sexualizing feet. Like why? It's feet! They are hardly the most attractive limb or body part that can be found, but then again to each their own, he supposed.

What had started as a lark, became a source of amusement and private entertainment for him. Ahmed was aware that it was a gross invasion of the privacy of these people, but he didn't intend to do anything with the things he found at first. Then he ran across a rather interesting account. This was the account of another local politician belonging to Sardar Bashir Farhan Shah -- a mouthful of a name it was. His name wasn't the only full thing about him. His bank account was massive. There was so much money in it that there was no way that at least some of it had not been collected by some nefarious means.

It would be so easy with all the information that Ahmed had just to take a small amount of it. Honestly, the man wouldn't even notice it he did, odds were half the time he didn't even check where his money was going.

So with a few simple steps, Ahmed had access to all his bank accounts, and he used that to make several small payments to dummy accounts that he had set up for another class project and then from there simply deposited the money into his account. Simple.

It had given him a bit of an adrenaline kick and just a little bit of a high. So, he had tried again a few months later, and then again just a few days ago. He succeeded each time, and each time Ahmed felt more confident in his ability not to get caught. He still hadn't told Adana and Liyana yet.

It was not a secret from them because he had said there was something that he was working on; he just hadn't said what it was precisely. Part of him was just a little bit apprehensive of their reactions because technically what he did was illegal, but it wasn't as if the three of them had never broken the law by hacking into something or the other, even if it was purely just for the fun of it. The difference this time was that instead of stealing an eBook or pirating a movie, he had stolen money from somebody.

Granted that somebody was a corrupt politician might not make a difference to his friends. He really hoped that he was wrong and that the two of them would take it in stride. He looked around, searching for his friends. He hadn't seen them enter the party yet, Liyana had said that she would be coming with Adana and that she would drive them both there, as Adana had left his car in the repair shop for the hundredth time just this year.

Ahmed wished that Adana would finally get a different car so that it would stop breaking down all the time. Maybe with all the money that he had collected from those hacked accounts, he could buy a car. It would certainly help his friend out and make some things easier for him. They lived together anyway, and it wouldn't be that hard to convince Adana that the car would benefit them both, as not to hurt his friend's pride.

Speak of the devil. Adana and Liyana had just walked into the party. As usual, Adana was underdressed in simple jeans and a band T-shirt, from this distance

Ahmed couldn't tell what group, but the odds were Led Zeppelin, Def leopard, or The Fray. Adana had a bit of an obsession with vintage band shirt T-shirts.

Liyana, on the other hand, was dressed to impress, which to be honest, was out of character for her. She was the kind of person who liked dressing comfortably; she would arrive dressed in sweatpants and a hoodie if she could get away with it. She had to be convinced most of the time to wear attire that was appropriate for the occasion. So, it was somewhat disconcerting to see her dressed so nicely without any pressure.

For a brief moment, Ahmed wondered if she was dressed that way because of a boy. He felt a moment of rage at the thought that she might have dressed up to impress another guy. He pushed back the feeling, he had no right to feel that way, she wasn't his girlfriend, and they weren't in the kind of relationship where he could dictate what she did or didn't wear and for whom.

"Liyana! Adana! Over here!" He shouted, hoping his voice would carry over the light music playing in the background. It must have because his friends looked in his direction just a moment later. With a smile, Ahmed made his way in their direction. They met halfway, and almost immediately, Liyana pulled him in for a hug. Ahmed felt his heart judder and skip a beat. It was over in a moment, and Adana was pulling him in for an arm shake and half hug.

"When did you get here?" Liyana asked, "you are usually so late to these things."

"Not long, I just arrived, and then you guys walked in," Ahmed said, as he turned toward the table that held some beverages. "What do you wanna drink?" He inquired, looking at Liyana.

"Anything is good, but no alcohol. I'm not really in the mood tonight."

"Why? Is everything

okay?"

"Yeah! Yeah! It's all good I just wanna stay sober, I have some things that I need to do tonight. I mean later tonight, so I'd like to stay sober." Liyana tilted her head as she pursed her lips.

"Sounds good! One virgin pina colada coming right up!" He smiled at Liyana. "And you Adana? Are you gonna make me drink alone tonight?"

Adana smiled good-naturedly before replying to his question. "As long as none of us have to drive home. I'm good with having a drink." With that statement

Adana took the drink that Ahmed offered him with a smile.

As the night progressed, without realizing it, Ahmed had indulged in one too many drinks and started to feel the effects. He stumbled and bumped into somebody. It was entirely accidental, and before he could get his wits together to apologize, the guy who he had accidentally jostled turned around and shoved him.

Ahmed wasn't sure if it was the alcohol, or the general frustration about Liyana that night, which triggered a rather violent response from him. Normally, he would have just walked away. After he regained his footing after being shoved, Ahmed let his fist loose punching the guy square in the face with a left hook.

"You fucking asshole!" The other boy screamed as his nose bled. With that insult, the guy tried to tackle him. Before he could make contact, his friends pulled him away with stuttered apologies and statements about their friends' drunken state. Then, the boys walked off although their friend didn't want to leave.

The whole way out he kept shouting profanities and screaming at Ahmed. In his anger, and with all the alcohol in his system, Ahmed followed them out. Lucky for him, Adana had taken notice of the commotion. and after leaving Liyana in the company of a reliable friend followed them out.

"Hey Ahmed man what are you doing?" Adana asked his friend, grabbing onto his arm to steady him as he stumbled out into the parking lot. "Why're you picking this fight? You don't even know these guys!"

"What do you mean, why? Didn't you see what he did?" Ahmed argued back.

"It was just a push. Don't make this into a bigger deal than it needs to be." Adana was trying to deescalate the situation by getting Ahmed to walk away; only his words didn't seem to be helping and were making Ahmed angrier.

"He disrespected me by pushing me, it was unprovoked. I was about to apologize for bumping into him!" Ahmed shouted; his already alcohol-flushed face turned redder from anger. "Yes! And you punched him, probably broke his nose. I would call that even." Adana tried to justify, hoping Ahmed would take the win and walk away.

I was too late, it looked like Ahmed had already decided he wanted to fight. When he was like this, there was no one who could talk him out of it.

If he hadn't been drunk, Adana might have tried to get Liyana to talk some sense into him, but honestly, he didn't want her to see the violence that was obviously going to follow if she failed.

"Fine, you do what you want, I'm gonna stand here and make sure you don't get yourself killed, but I'm not getting involved in this fight. Do you understand that?" Adana made one last-ditch effort to talk his friend out of this fight.

"Okay." With that one word, Ahmed walked in the direction toward the waiting guys.

Before long, a crowd had formed, with Ahmed and the boy Jamal. Adana had overheard his name, as his friends tried to talk him out of the fight as well. Looks like both of them had far too much damn pride - pointless pride - in Adana's opinion.

They had begun circling each other, like dogs. Both too far gone to realize how ridiculous they looked. The kept looking at each other to spot any sign of weakness. From the way they glared at each other and the stubborn look of determination on their faces, it was highly doubtful that either was ready to back down from a fight.

The first one to attack was Jamal. He threw a punch at
Ahmed it hit him on his cheek, making him stagger
back several feet before regaining his balance. Adana
flinched in sympathy as the fist made contact, for a
moment he considered stepping in to stop this before
it got worse. Before he could take a single step
forward to stop the fight, Ahmed lunged at Jamal with
a kick and a punch in quick succession. The kick
contacted his side, and as he leaned over to grab his
now injured abdomen, Ahmed punched him right in
the nose, which made a satisfying crunch as blood
spurted from it. The fight had only just begun when
the sound of gunshots reverberated, surprising
everyone breaking up the fight. Everyone scattered in
fear or took cover.

Adana looked around to see the source of the sound --
a man with a handgun clutched in his right hand,
standing by one of the parked cars. At this distance
Adana could not make out his features but determined
the man was of average height and build. The only
discerning thing about him was the fact that he had a
gun in his hand.

Adana felt chills ricochet down his spine. Something
about the man by the car seemed very, very off. He
wanted to grab Ahmed and run in the other
direction, just like everyone else had; however,

Adana was not a coward.

His father made it very clear what his expectations were of his son, and that included being the type of man who could handle himself in situations just like this. Adana learned early to stand his ground and fight and the wisdom of walking away from those he knew he could not win. It didn't take a genius to understand the man standing in front of them was one dangerous mother fucker, the guy practically oozed danger. They needed to leave, now.

Only Ahmed, in his infinite wisdom, decided that it was a good idea to walk in the direction of the Armed man. He debated for a moment whether he should just walk away, but years of loyalty, friendship, and a general concern for Ahmed's wellbeing made him follow. He briefly wondered if he would come to regret this decision.

"Hey! why the fuck did you do that?" Ahmed asked to the gunman.

Adana froze. "Great going, Ahmed. Insult the man who has a gun and is obviously not afraid to use it in public. Why don't you?"

"I would think that one would not respond with a thank you in a situation like this." The man's voice was chilling, he had a smile on his face, and what sounded like a hint of humor in his tone, but something about the delivery of that line made Adana apprehensive.

"Thank you? For what? Letting that asshole get away!" Ahmed countered.

"No, for saving your life, you nitwit. The guy you were just about to fight had come out here and shoved a blade up his sleeve. Odds were, he would have stabbed you in that fight. So, your welcome."

And with that statement, the gunman walked off.

"Hey! Aren't you gonna give me a name? You know so I can thank the guy who saved me," Ahmed said jokingly.

The guy turned around and looked Ahmed with a smirk. "Hakim," he said, using the barrel of his gun to salute at Ahmed before continuing to walk away.

"Now that's what I call badass," Ahmed declared as he watched Hakim leave.

"Badass! How drunk are you? That guy was terrifying! This is the last time I'm letting you get this drunk! Do you realize what could have happened? You could have died! Sometimes you're so bloody careless, and not just with your own safety but with mine and Liyana's! Anything could have happened today!"

Adana was angry, sometimes Ahmed could be so selfish. He often forgot that he wasn't the center of the universe and that things were happening outside of just what he could see and understand.

With that said, he didn't wait for Ahmed to respond. He was gonna take Liyana home, and then go sleep. Ahmed could take care of himself. He clearly didn't need Adana around, he always just ignored any advice he gave, and just did his own thing.

Chapter Six

Last night was a foggy blur in Ahmed's mind. So many things had happened. For the life of him, he could hardly remember what happened the night before. He had a vague recollection of arguing with a bunch of drunk students at a party, something or another about a gun, and then going home with a stranger because he couldn't find his car. As he looked around, he realized he wasn't at home and had slept on somebody's couch, but he didn't recognize the apartment. It was clearly nobody that he knew. He felt his face ache, he was most definitely bruised from the fight, and as he touched his face, it felt tender.

"So, I see Sleeping Beauty is finally woken up," an unfamiliar voice said.

He looked toward the direction of the voice to see who it was and recognized the face rather vaguely; he knew it from somewhere, but he wasn't sure where. It took a moment for his mind to clear enough for him to place the face.

"Hakim, right?" he asked, hoping he had gotten the name correct.

"Yeah that's me, nice

to see that you

remember."

"Oh, I see that your guest is awake. How much longer is he gonna crash in my apartment?" another voice asked. The owner of that voice was one of the scariest men that Ahmed had ever seen. He looked like he could crush his skull with a single squeeze of his massive meaty fists. "I'm Qadir, by the way, you're crashing my place," he added, gesturing to the apartment.

"I see, anybody wanna tell me how I got here? I can't remember a thing," he said, and then laughed.

72

"Sure, kid, do you wanna eat something first?"
Qadir asked. He was about to cook breakfast. It
wouldn't be too much work to add another egg or
two to the pan. It had been raining all night, luckily
the power hadn't gone out, but the odds were that
the streets would be flooded for at least a couple of
weeks now. Qadir wondered if all that rain was a
sign of things to come.

He made breakfast as Hakim, and the boy talked
about computers. He could barely understand
anything that they said, but they seem to be having a
lively conversation.

*Oh well, looks like the boy might stay awhile. Qadir,
broke another egg into the frying pan.*

***

Later That Same Day

Qadir plopped down on the couch after that boy
Ahmed left. "So did that go how you wanted it to?"
He asked Hakim. "He seems like a bit of an idiot to
me." He shrugged, not that Hakim would take
anything he said seriously, anyway.

"He might look like an idiot, and odds are he isn't very
street smart, but from what I have been told by

multiple sources the boy is a genius when it comes to complex algorithms and…"

Qadir cut him off, it was all computer gibberish to him, anyway. "…So, basically, the boy is your golden goose?"

"Yes, and I have every intention of ensuring that he does not get away from me," Hakim said with the kind of ruthless determination that made his so terrifying to all the people who met him. Qadir knew that he never wanted to be the object of Hakims fascination, it would never end well.

***

Three Months Later

"Danny, we need to talk to him about this! That guy oozes bad news practically every time he takes a step; we need to talk to Ahmed, he needs to stop hanging out with him. I can just feel it in my bones that something bad is about to happen."

"Don't you think you're being a bit dramatic?" Adana asked. "I mean it's only been a couple of months, to be honest, we don't really know the guy, you should give it a chance."

"You're always too optimistic about these things. This isn't a stray cat or dog that you could bring home; this is a person. A person that Ahmed is letting far too deeply into his life far too quickly. It gives me a bad feeling. I don't know what to do about it."

"Relax Lee, give it a couple of weeks. The novelty will wear off, and Ahmed will go back to being his normal self. Chill. If it starts getting worse, we'll talk to him. He's always willing to listen; at least sometimes." Adana laughed.

Liyana rolled her eyes. "If you say so, I do," she said.

"Fine I'll give it another few weeks, but then that's it I'm stepping in, Promise me you will too."

"I promise, I pinky swear." He laughed.

With a giggle, Liyana threw her pillow at him. He was probably right. She was overthinking this again, and it was hardly that big of a deal. In a few days, Ahmed would be back to his usual goofy self, and this whole thing would be behind them.

***

One Week Later

Lal Zaman was called out to help the River Police, he cursed and grumbled as he got out of bed and made his way to his car. He and all the other police who did not have an excessive caseload called in to help the River police. That squad was just another attempt by the city to default people into thinking that they were doing their job.

The River Police had not been needed in years since the River Ravi, had become dry and was no longer as large as it used to be. The city could barely justify having the squad around until today. In the last few days, it had rained so much the river overflowed. All the homes and buildings that had been built less than twenty feet from the river, were all experiencing unprecedented flooding. Nothing was going to be a genuine threat to life, but nevertheless, it was a severe annoyance to most people.

It was early in the morning, and for the first time in ten years, Lal Zaman could see people bathing in the river which had not happened in ages. The river had become too shallow and stagnant for people to swim in, not to mention that the lack of moving water also meant it just wasn't clean enough.

The poor of the city used to come to swim and enjoy the river with their families. Children jumped off the sides of the many bridges up and down the river. They dove and catapulted off the sides shouting with joy. Women cleaned the laundry, and the odd boatmen ferried people around in their rather dingily little boats.

The scene in front of Lal Zaman was exactly as it had been ten years ago. The whole point of the River Squad back then had been to police these people. According to the government, it was illegal to swim in the waters of this river. Lal thought it was rather stupid of the government to stop these people. Most of them could not afford running water to bathe or do laundry; they tried to save as much of their water as they could for drinking and cooking. The river was the only place they could come to bathe, do laundry, and at times socialise.

However, the residents around the river complained about the excess amount of people having picnics in their front lawns and making a mess of their gardens. So, the River Police had been created, which was another whim of the rich and powerful.

If those prissy rich folks ever had to go a single day trying to choose between drinking water or bathing for a week, they would understand why these people were here.

"All right, people! You've had your fun; it's time to move out!" his voice boomed in the quiet morning. The megaphone in his hand, enhancing it as he shouted out to the people trying to get them to evacuate before the stricter, less polite officers showed up and started shoving them into vans and arresting them.

"Come on, people, you're gonna get arrested!" Wow, Lal realised how incompetent he sounded when he said those things. It wasn't helping that all those people looked pitiful to him. The fact that he also didn't care if they moved added his lack of commitment to the cause. There wasn't anything that he had against these people.

He heard sirens in the background. The River Squad comprised of fewer desirable officers, then his own cybercrime squad arrived. These men hadn't done any real work in over a decade. Most of them had been used for crowd control during protests, or to barricade roads and provide security details when someone important visited the city, but the majority of their time spent sitting around in their squad room, on the other side of town. They were excited and overhyped. Mistakes are going to be made -- Lal didn't take charge of the situation.

He needed to find the man in charge of the squad and get him on his side, which was the only way this was going to work. *Fucking hell.* This was supposed to be his day off; he didn't want to work right now.

"Ah, I see you arrived. I've given these people a

twenty-minute warning to pack up; I don't want this to turn into a mess where the media. Besides, if we are seen being too rough we will just call trouble on to ourselves. We need to handle the situation peacefully," Lal said to whom he thought was the officer in charge. He sincerely hoped he hadn't made a mistake, because it would be so awkward if he had.

"That sounds alright to me," The man responded.

Lal could tell that he was also an Inspector, he wasn't obliged to take orders from him, but seeing that Lal had arrived at the scene first, he was now in charge.

"Okay, break up into groups and go up to these people and peacefully tell them to disperse if anyone tries to protest simply move on to the next group. We need to reduce the amount of the crowd before we take any kind of action where we have to arrest somebody. The fewer witnesses we have, the better if it becomes violent." Lal really hoped it wouldn't.

The men followed his orders breaking up into small groups to the trees as they made their way around the riverbank ordering people to disperse peacefully or be arrested. Most people nodded and started packing up. Stragglers near the end were intimidated into leaving by a simple show of force. Glad that the situation had been handled peacefully. Lal made his way do his Jeep and hopped in; he could probably use the rest of his free time catching up on sleep.

Chapter Seven

While swiveling at *Hussain Chowk* to save an undertaking scooter overloaded with what Lal Zaman could only assume was an entire generation of an extended family, he answered his superiors call on his police cell. He kept his eye on the traffic as he put the phone on speaker and tosses it on the seat next to him.

"Yes, sir *ji*, I'm looking into this...of course. Of course, *ji ji,* indeed sir *ji*, this case has been our department's full attention. I give you my word I'll personally present the culprit to you. Ok sir, thank you *ji, Allah hafiz ji.*"

Hanging up the phone, Lal Zaman muttered under his

breath, "*Haramda suddah... kutte dyaa...oyy!*" His train of thought was once again interrupted by the hectic Friday afternoon traffic in Lahore.

"Ughh," Lal Zaman sighed as he headed to his police station, wiping the sweat off his brow. This broken car AC was finally getting to him as June was approaching, but a malfunctioning second-hand police *dala* was the best that anyone in his precinct had, so complaining was out of the question.

With the tedious commute out of the way, what Lal Zaman needed now was a good cup of *chai*. Standing at the portable gas stove in the police stations 'kitchen' which also functioned as the prayer room and the back office where bribes were settled, he realized that his newest assignment was way out of his league.

It was dawning on him that he couldn't keep deflecting these dammed IT hack complaints to the prestigious 'National Center for Cyber Security' This new division had just been created to combat the growing number of cybercrimes happening in the country.

The problem was this new 'department' was nothing but a hoax. The City DC, under pressure from the elites, who were being hit the hardest with these attacks, had thrown together the NCS unit on a whim, and maybe too much television late one night. Now Lal Zaman was stuck managing a mishmash of officers from all over the place. Half of them were departmental rejects, and the rest were in trouble for one reason or the other.

The DC made it sound like it was going to revolutionize the way the police in the country were run and how they operated. The reality was far, far less glamorous. The new unit was stationed in a crumbling old Police building in the heart of Lahore. The building probably hadn't had occupants since the departure of the British, at the very least. It was falling apart, and every other day or some repairmen was fixing something, from the roof to the plumbing, it was all crumbling. Not to mention that the resources they were given. A half a dozen old Windows computers that took up two-thirds of the tiny desks they were given. The cars barely worked, the equipment was hardly of any use in catching cyber terrorists, and the building would collapse next time Sub Inspector Kamran from billing so much as sneezed in his basement office.

In general, the theme of the day, he also realized the milk he had added to his chai was rancid. Few exasperated sighs later, he called for the *chai wala;* his *chai* was awful, but at least it would be better than this rotten mess in front of him.

Now, if only he could solve this hacking problem as quickly as his *chai,* but there didn't seem to be any apparent solutions. Lal Zaman wasn't the best policeman in the city, but he also wasn't the worst. He showed up to work on time, didn't treat people under arrest badly, only beat the occasional idiot on the street, and had promised to only take bribes that he knew wouldn't in direct correlation mean that someone innocent would be harmed. He didn't mind the occasional traffic offender getting away or every other kid who had been caught with alcohol.

He took bribes like every other cop in the country, but he went about it with some conscious thoughts. Maybe this was just a case of bad luck. All those stupid things he had done coming to bite him in the ass.

Lal Zaman tried looking over at the papers on his desk again. Most of it looked like gibberish to him. He had no illusions about his ability to understand all the complexities and intricacies that went into coding and all this hacking-shmacking. All he wanted was for the paperwork to be in simple *Urdu*! Hell, at this point, he would take *Punjabi* anything was better than this gibberish of numbers and long, complicated English words. His grasp on the language was only rudimentary enough to fill out his paperwork and give the occasional lost tourist reliable directions, but that was where his expertise ended.

He needed someone who could understand this gibberish and then explain it to him and the men so that they could catch the people that were causing all this trouble. Once they were caught, the task force would be dismissed, and Lal could go back to solving typical crimes like robberies, runaway brides, and good old fratricide. Those were the simple days.

An idea occurred to him. He needed someone to translate and analyse all this paperwork, who better than an actual hacker. Lal knew just the man he could coerce into helping him. There was this petty thief turned hacker by the name of *Irfan Bhati* he owed Lal Zaman a favor for letting his brother go after he had been found in possession of jewelry from a recently burgled house. Irfan had promised his criminal service, limited though, they were to Lal when the occasion required it.

Now it was a matter of locating the man, which was just about as easy as looking for a rat in a swear, but Lal much preferred it to all this tech junk. Good old investigating was so much easier. He called for some of his officers.

"I need you to find someone. It's orders from above. The man's name is Irfan Bhati; he is in the system, he is a hacker and a thief, we got a tip that he could possibly be the man responsible for the recent climb in cyber-attacks. I'll have Officer Iqbal print out some pictures of him with his last known." He finished.

The four men in front of him proceeded to salute, after which he dismissed them and called in his secretary.

Allah Baksh Talpur was a small man. At five foot five, he was dwarfed by most of the men in the station as he scuttled about managing all the paperwork that the undersecretaries and the officers handed in.

With a neatly trimmed beard and round spectacles that always seeded to be slipping off his nose Allah Baksh hardly fit in at the station. He looked like he should be in front of a class of students; he seemed more like an academic with his tweed suits jackets and collection of ballpoints than a police secretary.

"Talpur, I need you to get everything we have on Irfan Bhati. I arrested him at one point for pickpocketing, so he should be in the system under my arrests. Get his picture and last known out to the men. I think we might have a possible lead on this damnable hacking business."

Talpur nodded as he made quick notes. One thing that could be said about the man, despite his appearance, was that he was more than adequate at his job. In fact, most of the officers in this precinct were good men. The problem was that these good men had at one point or another offended someone important and as punishment had ended up in this precinct as part of this ridicules cyber task force

Take Kamran from billing, the poor man was allergic to everything, and on one unfortunate day, after smelling some flowers seconds earlier, he had sneezed right into the open mouth of a sergeant. He had promptly been relegated to the basement of this precinct after that debacle.

Talpur had tried to report on an officer for stealing money from department accounts and had been hastily relegated to work for Lal. The stories continued in much the same fashion; Ali from homicide, Junaid from River Police, Kamal from Bomb Squad, and so on so forth. None of them were bad or incompetent officers; they just had bad luck.

Lal was sure that he could get them all out of this mess. His plan was not a sure-fire thing, but if it worked, they would all be able to move on. He was apprehensive but, at the same time, Lal hoped that his plan would work. If it did, it would mean they would get to move on from this hovel into a place where their expertise would come in handy. In the last few months, Lal had grown fond of the mismatched assortment of police officers who worked under him and as their superior officer, he wanted to do what he could to ensure that his men had a good future.

***

Two Months Later

Qadir was making his way to the pool hall. He hadn't been to that old haunt in almost three years now. He just didn't feel like going there. Six years ago, after Hakim had made his display of violence against the unnamed boy. It made Qadir sick to his stomach every time he went in. He had kept going until about three years ago. Someone there had been retelling the story to a friend, and just hearing it had soured the drink in Qadir's mouth. He had stopped going, and then soon after, had been in and out of prison a few times and just hadn't had cause to go back.

Now Hakim had invited him to the hall. He had no choice now he would have to go, or risk angering Hakim, and one should never provoke Hakim unless they have a bulletproof exit strategy for when things would go inevitably South.

As Qadir entered the pool hall, he found that nothing had changed in three years; the walls were still the same brown-stained mess he remembered, the same tiles were still sticky, and the bar was still the only piece of clean furniture in this place.

Hakim was waiting for him in the back. As usual, he was seated at his favorite table in the back with a glass of single malt whiskey that the bartender kept in stock just for him. He greeted Qadir with a nod and indicated for him to sit down. With great reluctance, Qadir sat down in the seat he was told to. He wanted to get up and walk out because he felt he didn't belong here anymore. He was not delusional enough to say that he was suddenly a changed man and would never commit another crime. He only wanted to get away from Hakim; he knew deep in his gut that this was going to end badly.

Hakim would joke with him that he had a way of weaseling his way out of trouble. It was not that he was good at getting out of trouble; he was just good at listening to that little voice that told him that something was going to go wrong. A woman he had been entangled with many years ago had said that it was probably a left-over evolutionary instinct, the lizard brain she called it. She had said something about it being his fight or flight instincts.

Too bad hers had been so underdeveloped. Qadir had left her quite damaged when he was done playing with her; she had been a loud one, and a fighter. Her instinct had been to fight him instead of running. Maybe if she had run, it would not have ended the way that it did. He was feeling himself get lost in his memory when Hakim spoke.

"We have a problem," Qadir's heart stopped. That was not good news. Not good news indeed, it was horrible news. He was almost afraid to ask what the problem was.

"Is there something I could do to fix it?" Maybe offering help would keep Hakim calm.

"Not unless you learn how to code in prison," Hakim replied gruffly, as he took a sip his whiskey. "I need a hacker, or more specifically someone who knows coding well enough to hack into something for me. That's what I was talking about yesterday. You know the guy, the one that studies at that school... You know the one I had recruited for this job. Well, that idiot went and got himself caught for something else." Hakim sighted.

"I see." Qadir said simply, too afraid to say more; there was no guessing at how Hakim would react in any given situation. The best solution was usually to keep quiet and let Hakim process his thoughts and come up with a plan. He always complained that people talked so much that he couldn't hear the voices in his head.

In Qadir's opinion, you shouldn't hear *any* voices in your head, except your own. And if you did, you probably shouldn't listen to what they say, much less do it. However, he kept that opinion to himself; he had some sense of self-preservation. He wasn't about to stick his hand into the lion's mouth for no good reason. After all, he had just gotten out of prison. There was no reason for him to provoke someone into sending him on his final journey prematurely.

"I need to find someone new, and I don't have a lot of options," he told Qadir. "I don't like working with someone I can't trust, or I haven't worked with before."

"The boy, the one who got arrested. Do you think he could give a reference for someone? You said he went to some type of tech school, right? So, the odds are that he would know a bunch of people that have the same, if not similar skills? He could vouch for them, and you could give them a trial run to see if you guys fit?" Qadir hoped that he wasn't about to get his head ripped off, both figuratively and literally. He waited. And waited. And waited.

"Hmmm," Hakim said, that was all. He didn't say anything further as he continued to sip his drink until it was finished and only spoke to ask for another one. They sat there in silence for a good ten minutes before Hakim finally spoke.

"That's not a bad idea. We can test out a bunch of people until we find one who fits. The only thing is we have a bit of a deadline to work with. We have until the end of next month to get this job done. I better find somebody to do it well, or there's gonna be a lot of trouble." He finished the rest of his drink in a single shot before standing. "I think I have someone to visit. I'll get back to you with the details." With that, he walked off, leaving Qadir confused. At least nothing particularly bad had happened.

Qadir finished off the water he had asked for, before finally leaving this wretched place behind.

***

Hakim made his way toward his car. As he slid into the driver's seat, he scanned his memories of the last few months. He needed to find someone else that could take this job. A name suddenly came to him. It was perfect. Why hadn't he thought of it before? The ideal person for the job had been staring at him for three months, and he hadn't even considered it.

As he pulled his car out of the parking spot, he pulled out his cell phone and scrolled down his contacts; there it was Ahmed Abbas. He was the perfect person for the job. He hit call. The bell rang twice before it was answered.

"Hello?" the voice replied groggily; it took Hakim a second to recall that it was 2:00 a.m. and that most people would be asleep by now.

"It's Hakim."

"Oh! Hey man! What's up? You good?" The voice

sounded a little bit more alert but still groggy.

"Yeah, I just need a favor."

"Sure, If I can I want to help, I owe you, right?" Ahmed laughed.

Perfect. Hakim thought. "Excellent, I can come by the house tomorrow morning and discuss it with you if you are available?" *He better fucking be available.*

"Yeah, sounds good. I'll be home all day. It's Wednesday, so I don't have any lectures, I have plans with Adana, but I can reschedule. I'll see you, then."

Ahmed acquiesced, "Good."

With that, Hakim hung up. That was one problem solved. Now he just had to make sure that the boy who got arrested didn't squeal. Irfan had such a loose tongue; he would need to be dealt with discreetly.

Chapter Eight

The next day, Ahmed was waiting for Hakim to arrive. In the last few months, the two of them had been spending a significant amount of time together. Both Liyana and Adana didn't like him; they continuously talked about the fact that he creeped them out, and Ahmed couldn't understand what they meant by that.

Sure, Hakim was odd, but he was hardly creepy. There was nothing particularly sinister about the man either, yet Liyana continuously nagged him about the time they spent together. She was always saying that he was a bad influence on him, which was so improbable, considering they had only known each other for about three months.

Yet both his best friends persisted insisting that Hakim was an unsuitable acquaintance and that Ahmed should distance himself from him. Truth be told, at first, Ahmed had taken their warning seriously, only to realize that they were entirely unfounded fears. Hakim was hardly a threat; he liked that Ahmed was a hacker, albeit not the greatest hacker, but he knew enough to keep things interesting. What was even more impressive was the fact that he had openly talked about using his hacking to siphon money from the accounts of wealthy politicians and industry moguls. This news had excited Ahmed; this was something that he was doing, albeit on a smaller scale.

From the things that Hakim described, it seemed like his operation was much larger and required more people. It was also much riskier because the money being siphoned was in larger quantities than anything that Ahmed would ever dream of taking.

The doorbell rang; it was Hakim. As Ahmed walked toward the front door to unlock it, he thought about the possibility that Hakim might be here to recruit him. A shot of excitement went through him at the prospect of being hired to work with Hakim.

He would make so much money; he might be able to help Adana finally quit tech University and do a degree in botany, and maybe even finally get up the courage to tell Liyana how he felt. Of course, this is all subjective, and he was just building castles in the sky without really knowing what was about to happen today. As he got closer to the door, a feeling came over him, he couldn't quite understand what that feeling was, but it seemed like a mixture between anticipation, excitement, and a gut-wrenching fear, all these emotions swirled and mixed around inside of him.

He opened the door to see Hakim. Ahmed always found it strange that even though Hakim wasn't very tall, his presence seemed very large. Ahmed always wondered how Hakim was able to hold himself up so well that it compensated for his lack of height. It made him a bit envious of the man. Ahmed was tall, yet he never could draw attention to himself the way that Hakim did. When Ahmed walked into the room, despite his height, he was often overlooked.

On the other hand, Hakim could walk into a room and command attention immediately. He was rather charismatic, with a hint of danger. It made people curious about the man drawing their attention to him.

"Aren't you going to invite me in? Are you gonna keep looking at me?" Hakim said.

Startled, Ahmed cleared out from the door. He had been staring at Hakim and blocking the door like a nitwit. "No! No! Of course, of course, come in" Ahmed said quickly. "I just thought you would come by a bit later, so I was surprised." He tried to cover up his faux pas.

"I see, I thought I texted you what time I was coming by?" Hakim said, eyebrow raised, and eyes filled with questions.

"Yes, ummm, you must have, I probably didn't read the text properly, my bad." Ahmed led him to the kitchen table, where he had prepared a small breakfast. "I had some tea made, would you like some?" he asked, hoping the ritualistic routine of having a guest over and giving them tea would calm him down. He couldn't understand why he felt so nervous; it wasn't like it was the first time that Hakim was coming over. He felt like he was being scrutinized very carefully; he just hoped that whatever test Hakim was giving him, he would pass it.

"Yes, thank you. I would like some tea." Hakim settled down into the chair and pulled the teacup closer to himself from across the table. "There are some things that I would like to discuss with you, and I would appreciate it if you gave me your full attention. It is important."

"Of course, you have my full attention," Ahmed said as he settled across from him, twining his fingers and holding his palms together, ready to listen.

"Well, it's come to my attention that you're a rather adept hacker." Hakim lifted his brow. "Some of your classmates who are of my acquaintance have told me that if there's anyone who can execute a flawless a stealth job, a simple in and out without leaving a trace, it would be you. Would you agree with that assessment?"

Ahmed was flabbergasted, he didn't know quite how to respond, this was it, this was the moment that he had been waiting forever since he found out what Hakim did for a living. He was being recruited. The only problem was he didn't know how to respond to the question. Would agreeing to the assessment seem too arrogant, or would disagreeing look weak?

He knew how much Hakim valued proficient and capable people; he was afraid that if he made it seem like he wasn't good at the job that Hakim wanted him to do, or if he came off as modest Hakim would simply find someone else. After all, it wasn't that hard to find hackers these days; it was an enthusiastic pastime of many young folks.

Hakim was still looking at him waiting for his answer, Ahmed didn't know how to respond, so he went with the truth. "I am a fairly good hacker, and my specialty is to install malware and data collection. So if those are the things that you need for this job, then I'm definitely your man. However, if it's something else, I don't know how well I would be able to do it without some prior knowledge or practice about what I'm gonna be up against." He finished nervously, hoping that Hakim didn't take offense.

"Not bad kid, you were honest, to the point, and you didn't over or undersell yourself. Now the only question is, how well do you work under pressure?" Ahmed laughed.

"Pretty well."

"Good, because there's gonna be a lot of pressure; you have about a month before the job starts, another month for the end of it. I'll bring the details by for you later. You go over them and tell me what you think. What can we do to improve the plans, and then we can come up with a game plan and execute it?"

"Sounds good. I'm ready," Ahmed said enthusiastically, and he really was ready. This was the moment they had been waiting for. If he did this well, it would mean so many things were going to be different. This was his chance to do something that would change his life.

Too often he had lived in the shadows of people—most of all his father. If things worked out for him in this job with Hakim, it would guarantee him the exact kind of independence that he had been craving for years from his father. His life now was too tightly controlled by that man, even though Ahmed was a grown man. This was it; this was his chance to change things for the better. He could not mess this up.

***

Later That Same Day

"They've been spending too much time together!" Liyana complained. "There's just something so off about him, I can't quite put my finger on it but just looking at him unnerves me."

"I know what you mean, I felt it the first time I saw him. I don't know why Ahmed doesn't see it or rather why he ignores it." Adana sounded equally frustrated. The two of them were so worried about Ahmed.

The last three months, he had been spending increasing amounts of time with Hakim. Neither Liyana nor Adana trusted the man. However, they couldn't get Ahmed to see what they saw.

"We have to figure out a way to get him away from Hakim long enough for Ahmed to understand, or we need to try to tell him. It feels like he is under some kind of spell. Everything he does and says doesn't sound quite like the old Ahmed all of it seems to be coming through this filter of Hakim." Liyana cried, so genuinely concerned about Ahmed's wellbeing, she didn't know what they could do to make him see what Hakim was really like.

"We need to talk to him one last time before he goes and does something stupid to impress Hakim," Adana said, as he squeezed her hand. They both sat worrying about the friend they both loved. He was walking down a dangerous path, and they could feel it.

Watching their friend step closer and closer to a cliff despite several warnings that it was there, was starting to take a toll on them all. Adana left to go see his parents, and Liyana was left alone to ponder what they should do about their friend. It was hard to watch him, and something needed to be done.

***

"You are home!" His mother's voice was full of surprise at seeing him. Adana glanced over at her. Kulsoom Abdullah was a small woman.

Adana greeted his mother with a smile.

"*Asalam u alikum Ami,* I wanted to come to see you. I was just missing you a lot. I wanted to know how you were doing."

His mother's face lit up with a smile. "*Wa-Alaikum-as-Salaam* son." She was now grinning from ear to ear. Her lovely brown face crinkling with joy as she looked at him. "I didn't know you would be home so soon. I thought maybe you would want to spend more time with Ahmed?" She said, almost hesitantly, almost as if she were afraid that he would disappear in an instant if she asked too many questions of him.

Adana felt guilty as he looked at her. She was caught between him and his father. They fought constantly, and she was stuck between the two most important men in her life. There was nothing Adana could do about the way that his mother thought.

Kulsoom had been taught from a very young age to be submissive and to hold her opinions to herself. Her marriage to Adana's father had not brought about any freedom from that; rather, it had bound her tighter with more constraints and rules.

"No, I wanted to spend the rest of the day with you, Ahmed can wait. I see him every day when I go home." He took a few steps forward and hugged his mother; she deserved better from him as her son. He breathed in the familiar smell of his mother.

Kulsoom was not a wasteful person, and would never spend money on herself, however her on indulgence was her perfume. She made it herself out of jasmine and a mix of other natural scents. It was a sweet and subtle smell, not overwhelming at all.

To Adana, it had always been a source of comfort. He had many memories of his mother, making the perfume over the years. He had diligently watched her as a child mesmerized by the way that simple flowers, twigs, bark, and a bunch of other seemingly miscellaneous items turned into something that smelled so wonderful.

As a child, Adana had sat outside in the garden with his mother surrounded by her tools and others sent making paraphernalia. She had measured things in beakers, used a pestle and mortar to crush things. Making infusions from barks and oils from flowers, she had worked slowly and with a steady hand.

Adana had developed an interest in botany from watching his mother. He would never tell his father that, of course, the man would only use it to blame his mother, and this would just become another thing they fought about.

"Have you eaten?" His mother's voice was muffled against Adana's chest. He still hadn't let go of her. With a small chuckle, he pulled back, still not letting go of her all the way. He was lucky to have both his parents in his life full time, despite how dysfunctional his family was.

Both Ahmed and Liyana had a hard time with their parents being separated and widowed, respectively. He needed to treat his mother better. He had to make things better for her by getting along with his father. That was the only way he could make her happy.

"No I wanted to eat with you," he said.

She gave him another one of her big smiles, and he felt his heart squeeze with guilt again.

"I'll whip something up for you." She hugged him back before she stepped back. "Would you like to eat in the garden? I just had tea there, so the table is set, and the weather is quite nice today as well."

He nodded to her as she made her way to the kitchen; she was practically buzzing with happiness at the prospect of him being home for dinner. It was both sad and endearing at the same time.

He would be a better son to her. He had the rest of his life to make up for all his shortcomings. He vowed to himself to make more of an effort to be better, to make more of an effort, it would be the least he could do. He had protected Ahmed for years. It was time for him to take more time to protect a person he loved but had neglected for years. In a lot of ways, he was all she had.

"I will be a good son," he whispered before making his way up to change into something more comfortable. After he had changed as he sat in the garden, he thought back on all the times in his childhood that he, Ahmed, and Liyana had run around in the garden.

The garden changed every year as his mother planted different types of flowers and changed the garden beds around. She would plant different annual flowers to go along with all her perennials. It was late summer now, and some of the flowers had already bloomed and faded, as autumn fast approached.

The daffodils and bluebells had long faded, but how

the marigolds were out. Soon the tulips would be in full bloom, already Adana could see their buds. The daffodils seed pods had turned brown and were ready for harvest. He could see his mother had marked the most promising of the flowers with gauze and ribbon and would soon be attaching small pouches around the seed pod to collect the seeds when the pods burst.

"Admiring my handy work, I see," his mother said with a soft chuckle as she sat down.

"Well, it deserves that and more."

"You always were my favorite

son," she said with a half-

smile.

He laughed. "I'm your only

son so that hardly counts."

"And that's why you're my favorite." She laughed, and he joined her.

He squeezed her hand. "It really does look amazing, mum."

His mother was an avid gardener, and Adana got his

green thumb from her.

There were houseplants everywhere indoors. His father believed that they were another extension of his mother's garden. That was not true, those plants were all his, and his mother, and he shared the secret. If his father ever learned that he was indulging in what he believed to be a very un-manly activity, he would disown him, but not before making him watch as he ripped the plants apart.

With a sigh, Adana waited for his mother to bring him some food. Today had been stressful enough as it was. He just wanted to get some food, sit, and talk about plants with his mother and admire the small paradise that she had created in her garden.

Chapter Nine

Liyana had decided to go to Ahmed's house. She needed to take the chance to tell him one last time that Hakim was the wrong kind of company. She was hoping that by some miracle, Ahmed would listen to her today. Liyana was aware that it was a long shot, Ahmed was a very stubborn person, and when he got his mind made up about something a certain way, it was hard to dissuade him of that notion.

She and Adana have been trying for weeks now; neither of them had had much success at convincing Ahmed that Hakim was bad news. The problem was that Ahmed was fascinated by Hakim and had no intention of not continuing the friendship between the two.

As she approached the house, Liyana took a moment to gather her thoughts and to think of the words she wanted to say. She had some idea of what she wanted to say to Ahmed; she hoped that these were things that could convince him that Hakim was not who he seemed. Both she and Adana had decided that it would be better if they spoke to him one at a time instead of ambushing him. Knowing Ahmed, if they talked to him together, he might think of it as an attack, as opposed to them trying to help him.

"Okay, Liyana, you can do this." Liyana gave herself a short pep talk in hopes that she could keep her confidence up. Without so much as a knock, as she already had keys, she walked in.

A stranger was sitting in Ahmed's kitchen table. He was rather easily recognizable because he had a very distinctive scar on his cheek. The rough look of him and his clothes became abundantly clear that this man was, in all likelihood, a friend of Hakim's.

"Hey, beautiful, are you lost?" The man had a raspy voice, and Liyana felt a moment of disgust at the way he was looking at her. This was just another example of how both she and Adana had picked up something sinister about Hakim, yet Ahmed had been unable to do the same.

"Who are you?" she asked, startled by the fact that a stranger was sitting in Ahmed's house. Her uneasiness about the way he was looking at her increased. She couldn't quite put her finger on it, but there was something very sinister in the way that he stared at her.

It was the kind of gaze that one would expect from a viper as it watched the mouse before it struck, it was the gaze of a predator stocking its prey. It gave her chills. Liyana had never really felt afraid of a man before. As someone who was brought up by a single mother, and with two guys as her best friends from the moment she had been able to walk, Liyana had been taught how to take care of herself.

In that moment, she could almost tell that even if she tried to fight, this person was probably too strong for her to make much progress against on her own. She looked around to see where Ahmed could be and realized that the French windows in the kitchen were open, which could only mean that Ahmed was outside on the balcony overlooking the garden. He must be having lunch.

The man at the table stood up and began to walk toward her, and Leisurely he began to circle her, running his gaze up and down her body. Deliberately he gave his lips a lick. She held back a shiver, showing him how he was affecting her would mean letting him; she would not give him the pleasure of seeing that he had unnerved her.

"Come now, gorgeous, tell me who you are? You know what they say, you are only strangers until you give out your name." He was trying to be charming and failing miserably; there was nothing remotely charming about the predatory way he was looking at her. Liyana felt a moment of genuine panic, as she realized she might be alone in the house with him.

"Hello? Ahmed are you home?" she called out, she felt instant relief as she saw the stranger had returned to his seat and Ahmed poked his head out through the open door.

"Oh! Hello Liyana, I didn't know you were coming by; how are you?" Ahmed asked. "Is everything alright?" He enquired as he moved into the kitchen from the porch where he must have been standing. As he approached, Liyana realized that the man at the table wasn't the only one in the house. As Ahmed saw her glance at the man at the table again, Ahmed introduced him. "This is Qadir; he is a friend of a friend."

Qadir gave her a small mocking wave.

She ignored it. It only took her a moment to conclude that the third person in the house was Hakim. The surge of anger at the fact the Ahmed was so dense threatened to consume her. Why was it that he couldn't see you so clearly happening before his eyes? "Ahmed, do you think it's alright if I can talk to you alone for a minute?" Liyana said hesitantly; she was hoping he would not turn her down.

"Yes, of course." Ahmed said as he put the dossier, he had in his hand, on the table in front of where the scarred man was seated.

"What did you wanna talk about?" Ahmed asked as they moved away from the kitchen and into the guest bedroom.

"Well... Thing is... I don't know how to start. Actually, I do know where to start, but I'm afraid that you won't like what I have to say." Liyana started very hesitantly. She felt like she was taking a risk confronting him with this head-on, but the fact was, this was the only way to go about it. Adana and she had already tried being subtle about their feelings and opinions about Ahmed's new friends, and it hadn't worked at all. Liyana would need to be blunt.

It was the only way that this was going to work. If she tried babying him or indulging him, it wouldn't do him any good; it would just harm him.

"Both Adana and I have been talking recently about the fact that you've been spending a lot of time with Hakim. Neither Adana nor I feel as if that is the right choice for you."

"Are you being serious?" He slid his fingers through his hair.

"Yes, of course, I'm being serious. Does this sound like something that Danny or I would joke about? We truly believe, and I do mean this truly believe, that Hakim is a bad influence on you. We think that maybe it would be a smart decision if you distance yourself from him." That was all Liyana managed to say, before he interrupted her.

"I don't get it! Why the fuck do you and Danny hate him so much? I don't understand what you have against him. He's not that bad. Sure, he looks rather unsavory at times, but really, why judge a book by the cover? ...Are you... You can't... Neither of you has given him any real chance. All you and Adana do is complain about him. Why can't you take a moment to get to know the guy. Once you do, you'll realize that he isn't that bad." Ahmed was getting more and more worked up as he paced across the room while he spoke to her.

She was worried that by him raising his voice, the men in the other room would hear them arguing. She did not want to get them involved in this. The last thing she needed was an audience to edge Ahmed on in this fight.

She interpreted him before he could get anymore worked up. She needed to back track this conversation before it got out of control. She softened her tone and lowered her voice. "Ahmed, we don't hate Hakim, I just think that being around him is changing the way that you think about certain issues and that worries me, that's all." She ended the statement with an imploring look. He needed to understand what was happening, and the possibility of what could happen if Ahmed continued down the path that he was taking.

"I know you and Adana are worried. And trust me when I say that I appreciate the fact that you guys care so much about me." Ahmed's tone was softer too, and he rested his palms on Liyana's shoulders. "But, I'm old enough to make decisions about the people who I spend time with, and what I do in that time with them is also my concern and no one else's.

Do you understand?" His tone was so calm and so reasonable that for a moment, Liyana was almost convinced that he was right.

There was no talking to him. Not while he was still so firmly in the grips of Hakim. Whatever the man had said to Ahmed had him convinced that Hakim could say no wrong and do no wrong. Liyana had done all that she could do short of physically dragging her friend away from Hakim.

The new man Qadir worried her too, but despite his obvious provocateur behavior, she was well aware of who the real threat was. Liyana knew that she had done all she could do to convince Ahmed that a continued acquaintance with Hakim could only lead to disaster. Ahmed would have to learn the rest for himself.

She told her friend goodbye and hoped to God she had made the right decision in not having Adana carry him off somewhere and lock him up until the threat of Hakim had passed, and they were all out from under his large and suffocating shadow.

***

Later That Night

Liyana woke up to a strange sound. Someone was

moving around in the house. It wasn't her mum.
Once her mother took her sleeping pills, she was out
like a rock for seven to eight hours straight. The clock
on her nightstand told her that the time was 3:15
a.m. It was not her mother; they didn't have any
pets, and no one else lived in the house.

Liyana took a moment to get her bearings. She looked
around her room. The soft pastel blues and greens of
her bedroom were masked in lovely dove grey from
the light from the moon. It shone through her
window, creating shadows. The mountains and
valleys of dark shadows of varying darkness and size
filled her room. She flipped on the light, and the
room was bathed in a warm yellow glow as the lamp
illuminated the room, chasing away the wispy
shadows.

She didn't know if she should get out of bed or
continue to lay there and pretend to be asleep. If it
were a burglar, the odds were they would take what
they wanted, and they would be on their way. If she
stayed quiet, there was a good chance the burglar
would leave without ever knowing that she had
woken up.

Most burglars didn't go around killing the people that
they were robbing. Murder attracted far more police

attention and scrutiny than a few stolen necklaces. The smart decision would be to stay quiet; so, she did. Liyana waited for all the sounds to stop. She heard the burglar creeping around all over the house. She was afraid that they would come into her room and realize she was awake.

She felt like she was paralyzed in her bed. For a moment, she considered the horrifying thought that the person who had broken into the house was that awful man she had met at Ahmed's. She didn't want to think of the consequences of the fact that it might be him. She was not naïve enough not to recognize the terrifying things that had been playing out behind his eyes as he circled her.

She did not doubt that if she had truly been alone at that moment in Ahmed's house, that encounter would have ended very differently. The fear that her mother might be hurt prompted her to leave her bed. She reached under the bed and pulled out a baton, which was the only thing still left from her brief and rather unsuccessful time in the world of competitive gymnastics. Ahmed and Adana had been extremely supportive of her desertion. It had lasted until they saw her perform. They had quickly talked her out of it. They said she was better off with them in Krav Maga and Kendo.

Her bamboo Kendo sword was downstairs in the home gym; the baton would buy her time until she could get help. With a slow breath to calm herself, she needed to stay calm if she was going to do this. Being nervous and scared would mean that she would make mistakes. She couldn't afford to do that right now.

The hallway light outside her room was lit; anyone coming up would cast a shadow that would betray their presence to her. She flipped her lamp closed. She needed to have the advantage here; the intruder should not know that she was awake.

Trying not to make a sound, she called Adana and texted him at the same time. He picked up the phone, texting him to come over, and then she hung up. After sending him another text saying SOS, the paranoid friends that they were, they had come up with a way to contact each other when there was a real emergency. They had only used it once before when Ahmed had gotten tangled up with some rather dangerous people, while he had been away at boarding school for a year.

She and Adana had helped him out of that rather unfortunate scrape with only a minimal number of cuts and bruises. Heart beating as fast as a hummingbird and palms slick with sweat, she made her way out of her room. She was sure she was about to run into someone at every corner she turned, but with every light she turned on and as every dark corner was passed without incident, she got calmer. At the last door, she was so sure she was going to run into the intruder.

That never happened, the burglar finished what they were doing and had disappeared.

Twenty minutes later, Liyana felt calmer. Adana had arrived and was with her as she checked the house for the second time. He walked in front of her like a wall of protection. Liyana felt a surge of love for her best friend. She could always count on Adana to be there.

Soon, it became clear that the burglar had not taken anything. They had obviously been in the house as drawers were open and disturbed, the backdoor lock had been broken, and that was the entry point. The fact that while the house had been searched, nothing had been taken only added to Liyana's suspicions that this was Qadir. There were two scenarios as to why he had broken into the house today, if it was, in fact, Qadir. First, he had been trying to scare her so she would stop trying to convince Ahmed to ditch Qadir and Hakim.

The second, more terrifying reason was that he had come to hurt her or her mother. This was just as likely as the first scenario, but Liyana hoped it was not true, a deranged stalker was the last thing that she needed right now.

Adana slept on the couch in the living room. He left early in the morning after he was sure that everything was okay. They didn't tell Hinna anything; they didn't want her to worry about anything. Liyana had shared her suspensions about who she believed had broken into the house. Adana had been furious; he was ready to attack the guy, but Liyana had talked him out of it.

They could not risk it; if it had not been Qadir, they would further alienate Ahmed. At this point, Adana was willing to risk it, this involved the safety of someone so important to him, and Ahmed was digging his own hole at this point. Adana did not want himself and Liyana to be dragged into this any further. However, for her sake, he decided to hold off on the accusations. He just hoped that he would not come to regret this choice that they were making.

Part of Adana wanted to barge in Ahmed's house and knock some sense into him. Ever since this whole mess with Hakim had started to become something that looked somewhat like a permeant fixture, Adana had moved out of the home he shared with Ahmed.

For a month now, he had been living with another friend; he did not want to get his parents involved because that was a sure-fire way of getting Ahmed's father involved in the matter, and honestly, that was the last thing that would make this situation better. In fact, it was more likely to blow it up even more and make it worse.

Chapter Ten

One Month Later

He couldn't believe it. He had done it. Ahmed had just managed to steal five million dollars. He was set for life. Hell his grandchildren would be set for life. She would never have to work again. He had managed to score big. As far as Hakim, he didn't know that Ahmed had managed to crack the firewall around the MPs computer. he was still waiting for Emma to report back on his progress.

The truth of the matter was he had no intention of

doing so. In the last month or so, Ahmed had worked like a dog, day in and day in and day out, continuing to design malware after malware hoping to find a chink in the armor. That was the MPs computer. Whoever had designed it, had planned it very well. They had thought of almost every possible scenario, virus, malware, phishing email known to man. It had taken Ahmed More than three weeks to create a custom virus for the MPs computer.

The MP, also known as *Fahad Ali Abbasi*, Was a bit of an anomaly. He hardly had any social media accounts. His public email was managed by his assistant on a government-issued laptop, and his personal email and personal device used a closed network. He was meticulous not to open any emails or documents on his personal computer that were related to official business. He was also very old fashioned about the way he spent his money.

He kept detailed account books in analog form; he used checks to pay for things, never owned a credit card, didn't use online banking, and hardly ever spent money frivolously. His defenses had seemed imprint impenetrable. Until one day, Ahmed had found a weakness.

Mr. Abbasi had a twelve-year-old daughter, who

absolutely loved to play barbs games. It only took a few well-placed ads for a fake new game popping up on her feed for a few days for her to install the app. As her tablet shared the same closed network as her father's phones and computer, Ahmed now had access to all his personal documents.

What he found astounded him. This man who they had been watching for nearly a month thinking he would have maybe $1,000,000, turned out to have five stashed away.

Ahmed was beyond ecstatic. With this money there was just about nothing that he couldn't do. He would simply tell Hakim that he failed to hack the account and that he could find no way to penetrate the defenses of the security system, simple. Hakim had enough knowledge about the system and had seen Ahmed try to hack it for over a month now every time it wouldn't be that hard to convince him that he had failed once again. Once a sufficient amount of time had passed, he would start spending the money.

The first thing he was gonna do was by a car for Adana. After that, he was going to take Liyana out for dinner and tell her how he felt. It was going to be perfect. He had the restaurant picked out; it was *The Flaming Giraffe'* in *Gulberg.* Liyana had wanted to eat at that restaurant the day it had opened; however, the food was crazy expensive, and impossible to obtain a reservation unless you knew somebody. However, if you had enough money, anything was possible; and now, Ahmed had more than enough to do just about anything that he ever wanted to.

 He was gonna get his mom, the best divorce attorney in the country so that she could finally end her separation and finally get a divorce from his father without losing everything. His life would be different now, and he would be less selfish and try to remember and be grateful for all the people in his life. This was the moment where he was gonna make a big change.

***

Two Weeks Later

Tonight he would give Adana the car and take Liyana out for dinner. He knew he should have waited a bit longer before spending any of the money that he had gotten from the account, but he thought that Hakim had moved to a different city, and it would be fine if he started spending the money. Plus, if he went any longer without telling Liyana how he felt, his feelings would implode.

He had waited years for the perfect opportunity to tell her how he felt, and now he had that trinity, he wasn't gonna waste this chance. He planned everything down to the last detail so that he could be with the woman that he loved.

The night started out quite great. He had managed to convince Adana and Liyana to come out to dinner with him informing them that there was something important that he wanted to discuss with them. He realized that his behavior in the last few months had been deplorable, but it had been necessary as he needed to convince Hakim that he was indeed under his power. And what better way to do that, than to show him that he was willing to give up his best friends. It all was a lie, of course, but nobody knew that.; not even Adana and Liyana so he could imagine how hurt they had been by what they could only assume was a genuine reaction. He had hurt his friends deeply, and now he needed to fix that.

Liyana arrived first. She was dressed simply in a *kameez* and trousers. The lovely lemon color of the *kameez*, made her creamy skin and pink cheeks stand out all the more. She looked absolutely stunning in his eyes, and in Ahmed's opinion, there was no one more beautiful, kind, compassionate, and loving Liyana.

"Hello," he said softly. He watched as she pursed her lips, she did not greet him back. His heart sank, perhaps she was a lot angrier than hit first thought. If that was true, then he was in some real trouble. He didn't know how he was going to convince her that it was not all his fault.

He needed her to be okay with him, or all this would have been in vain. Perhaps he should start with Adana tonight and confess to Liyana when they were alone.

Liyana took the seat across from him even though he had gotten up to pull out the chair beside him. They waited in silence until Adana arrived; the silence was almost deafening. Neither of them were ready to talk about anything nor willing to be the first to compromise. Both of them for being stubborn, but Ahmed realized most of what had happened had been his fault.

"I wanted to take this chance to explain everything to both of you, do you know if Adana will show up?" He paused as she stared at him. "He hasn't replied to any of my texts, so I don't know if Danny's gonna be here today. I want him to hear this from me as well." Ahmed tried to explain.

It was somewhat futile, Liyana had already made up her mind. She was in no mood to listen to any of his excuses, his apologies, or his confessions. She and Adana had spent the last month and a half agonizing over the decisions that had been made. Their best friend had treated them both like dirt, ignored their opinions, dismissed their advice, and replaced them with a bunch of thugs.

Adana might be more forgiving than her, but Liyana had no illusions about the kind of man who Ahmed was. No matter what reasons he gave, nothing would excuse the behavior that she and Adana had to deal with since Ahmed met Hikam almost five months ago. Maybe there had been a chance earlier; however, after the way that Ahmed had ignored them in the last three weeks, in Liyana's opinion there was no going back.

"He will be here; he's just running a bit late. There were a few things he needed to take care of, so I let him borrow my car."

"Oh, I see, and how did you get here if he has your car mean?"

"I took an Uber, they're pretty reliable." That almost felt like an indirect jab toward him, but he couldn't be sure if it was intentional or he was just oversensitive. He had fucked up quite a bit in the last few months, hopefully, his friends would find it in their hearts to forgive him. Afterall, they were all he had.

Adana entered the restaurant. He looked content,

mostly happy with himself. The last month or two without Ahmed present all the time like he had been for most of Adana's life, he had felt a sense of freedom. Something he hadn't really felt before especially because he was always running around, trying to solve problems that Ahmed had created. He never had enough time for himself or things that he liked to do. The last few weeks had been a blessing because they allowed him to pursue the things that he loved.

He also came to the realization he didn't need to be around Ahmed 24/7 to feel like he was accomplishing something; he was quite capable of doing that himself. Whether that was sitting down to paint, play Scrabble with his grandmother, or play *Call of Duty* with Liyana. His life contained far more than just Ahmed. It was high time he realized his life didn't need to revolve around his friends. He was his own person, and he had every right to experience his own life.

"I wanted to talk to the two of you, there were things that I did that I regret, and things that I said. I realized that I hurt the both of you very badly. I also realized that you don't need to forgive me, as much as I would appreciate it. I've also come to realize something else; I need the two of you more than you need me. You guys are the glue that holds me together, without the two of you in my life, I feel like I might float away like an untethered balloon. He was nervous, and terrified that he was about to be rejected. He didn't know how he was going to go about this. He only knew he needed to tell his friends everything that had happened, but I didn't know where to start.

If he told them that he had done the things that he did because he wanted the money, they would never forgive him, but he saw no other way out of it. So he told them everything. He told them how after that night at the party, Hakim had met him again at the university the next day, how they had started hanging, what Hakim had wanted him to do, what he had done, how he had lied to Hakim, how he maneuvered him out of the money leaving him without a single penny. He apologized to Liyana because she had to meet Qadir and he apologized to Adana for all the rude things he had said to him after the party.

The two of them listened to everything that he had to say. However, neither of them forgave him. They felt abused and used, they had been placed on a chessboard like pawns, moved around without their consent, their feelings manipulated, their emotions played with and their friendship permanently damaged.

They rose to leave as Ahmed tried to stop them to no avail. "Please, guys, please just listen to me. I know what I did was wrong, but just please give me a chance!"

She scolded, "No, what you did was despicable. You used us. You used decades of our relationship, of our trust. For what? Money? That's not a good enough answer, Ahmed. No amount of money is worth what you did. I hope it gives you comfort in the long nights and days to come because neither Danny nor I have any interest in ever speaking to you again." With that last statement, Liyana walked off.

Ahmed was crushed; the grief in his heart raged. He didn't know what to do.

He heard a familiar voice. "So, that was your plan, I see. Rather rudimentary don't you think, still effective, you managed to fool me for a while. However, your fool ass couldn't wait a few more months to spend that money. I would've been cities away if you'd just waited a little longer, unlucky for you friend of mine. How are you doing? Give me a little call. Looks like I'm the one with all the cards now motherfucker!" Hakim was here.

Ahmed froze. His face filled with terror as he realised that he was well and truly fucked. There was no getting out of this. Hakim had caught him red-handed about to spend his money. There was no way that he was going to get away scot-free. He was going to have to pay the piper, so to speak. He just hoped that Hakim was feeling generous and would not rip him to shreds.

***

Lal Zaman had been woken up from his sleep by a frantic secretary. He was told that Irfan was at the police station and was ready to confess to everything that had happened. He had rushed to the station in hopes of confronting the man. In the last few months they had worked with him, he had deciphered all the information that they asked of him. However, he had refused multiple times to tell them who was responsible for these attacks.

All he would say, was that the man was a monster. The monster who would kill him, his family, and anybody he cared about if he ever spoke his name. So, when Lal Zaman got the news the man was ready to confess, he rushed over immediately.

In the next hour or so, Irfan told them everything. How he had been recruited by a man called Hakim

Omar. How this man had manipulated, coerced, and threatened his way to power in the criminal underground. Every petty criminal knew who he was, they all might not know what he looked like, but they recognized the name immediately. There was no running or hiding from this.

As Irfan told his story, Lal Zaman planned how he would catch this man.

"The main thing that you have to understand about Hakim is that he's not scared of anything. Most people have some kind of rational or irrational fears; hell, most people are scared of something. Hakim isn't scared of anything. Sometimes, when you look at him, you get this feeling that you're staring into a bottomless pit of darkness, and that pestering back you ready to pull you in," Irfan said.

"Sounds a bit excessive, don't you think? He is just a man." Lal tried to reason.

"Oh, I know he's a man, that's what makes him so terrifying. He's a monster. Whoever he found to replace me, they fucked up big time. The rumours going around is that Hakim got screwed over by some college boy. He took all of Hakim's money and ran off." Irfan stopped to drink some water his handcuffs clinked, rattling as he moved the chains attached to reach for the glass of water in front of him. As he took a sip, Lal watched him shiver as if every memory of this man terrified him.

Things were starting to add up. This was the reason that he had been unable to find the guy. No one was brave enough to talk about the man. He was a phantom, Iblis, and a nightmare all rolled into one as far as these people were concerned. He had obviously done enough to scare these hardened criminals into not speaking about him to anyone.

Lal had learned to take criminals seriously when they said they were scared of another person. Most of the time, if they admitted something like that, Lal was sure he was dealing with a sociopath of one kind or another. Someone charismatics enough to be able to pass amongst people, and yet still sufficiently terrifying to inspire fear from the people he encountered.

He listened to everything that he said carefully; he was going to catch this man.

Chapter Eleven

It was all over. There was no going back now. He had been caught, Hakim knew everything, how he had lied. Hakim was going to kill him.

Hakim had driven him just outside the city. Like a fucking idiot, he had gone along with him like he did not know what was about to happen to him. He was not an idiot, but apparently, he had lost a few brain cells out of fear.

It was very clear that Hakim had every intention of killing him. There was no saving him now. No one was going to come and rescue him from this nightmare. He was prepared to beg Hakim for his life, which was probably the only choice that he had at this point.

"Hakim, please listen to me. I'm so sorry; I shouldn't have done this. But you need to understand it was just a mistake. I wasn't trying to disrespect you. I swear I'm gonna return the money to you. Just give me a computer and five minutes, and I'll give you all the money." Ahmed was shivering now. He was afraid he would lose control of himself. There was no getting out of this.

"Oh, you fucking idiot!" Hakim laughed. "Do you think it's going to be so easy? There is no way that you are going to get out of this." He pulled the car to a stop. He pulled Ahmed out of the car. Ahmed tumbled out, pulled on by the momentum. He was shoved in on the ground as Hakim pulled out his gun from behind his back.

Ahmed crawled onto his knees. He was terrified now. Hakim was not listening to him at all now. He had a crazed look in his eyes. There was this strange fire burning behind his eyes. He was going to kill him, of this Ahmed had no doubt. He just hoped that however it happened it was quick.

It was not quick, and it was not painless.

Hakim took his time, after shooting him in both legs so that he was immobile, Hakim pulled out a blade. Even with all the pain he was feeling, Ahmed knew it was not the worst of what was to come. Things were about to get a whole lot worse. In fact this was in no way over. The pain was only just starting. Hakim was going to do some very, very bad things to him before it was all over.

Hakim brought the blade down toward his eye. Ahmed felt the tip of the blade enter. It burned. He was aware that the metal of the knife was likely cool, but to him, it felt like it had just been pulled out a fire and was jammed into his eye. He could hear inhuman screaming, and for a moment, he wondered who else was there. It took him a while to realise that the screaming was him. He only became aware of the fact when he realised his throat felt hoarse. He didn't know in what sequence the next few things happened. All he remembered was pain. He pissed himself as he shivered in pain. The blade was used to cut away his shirt before Hakim ran it over his skin. He increased and decreased the pressure of the knife cutting his skin at varying depths. At some point, he was stabbed in the thigh. Hakim had his hands around his throat choking him. This was the end. He could tell.

His last thoughts were of Liyana as the darkness closed in around him.

***

Hakim used Ahmed's Phone after he had killed him to text his friends. He had killed him in a rather simplistic manner. He had simply strangled him. It was quick and to the point. However, he had done so many other things before he killed him.

There was a certain kind of pleasure in watching someone slowly come to the realization that they were about to die. He had not come to that conclusion quickly. For all his smarts, Ahmed was an idiot, even to the very last second begging for his life. He had giving Hakim all the information that he had asked of him. He had cried and begged until the very end for his life. Hakim had created a rather large mess; it would require help to clean up. He called up Qadir to come to meet him.

Adana and Liyana responded to the text immediately. They came rushing over even though they had just fought with their friend only an hour ago. Their stupid loyalty is what had gotten them into this mess, and now they would die because of it. Hakim was ready; he was standing by to kill them; with all the rain recent rain the *Ravi* River had overflown, creating shallow graves by its banks would be fairly easy as the soil was soft from all the water.

The time it took for the bodies to be discovered would be enough for Hakim to escape. It was good enough. He didn't take his time killing them; he was quick, efficient, and clean. He killed them both with a single stab through the under the rib right into the heart. It was instant death. Well, maybe not immediate as blood filled in the lungs, and they slowly bled out internally, it was undoubtedly a sure death if not a quick one. It was good enough.

The girl had fought, hard. She managed to scratch his face and rip his shirt before he was able to stab her. He almost wished he could have kept her alive to play with. She would have been fun to play with. Her spirit was the kind that would have kept him entertained him for weeks.

Qadir had cried the whole time while burying her. Hakim had left him to bury her. He needed to leave town immediately, a triple homicide of three, wealthy students would bring too much heat. He had more than enough money to hide and not be caught.

***

Just hours later, Lal Zaman and a squad of undercover cops were waiting at the pool hall, ready to ambush Qadir and Hakim when they came in. However, Hakim was long gone. He had run off right after burying the bodies. In his confusion, grief, and horror, Qadir had ended up stumbling into the pool hall only to be caught by Lal Zaman.

Qadir had wanted to a drink after having one of the worst days of his life. However, it was not over. The second he had walked into the Hall, he had been ambushed and was taking into custody, he had lost his freedom all because he had been foolish enough to help Hakim out.

It was a clean, quick operation. With no casualties, a small task force of mismatched cops, had caught one of the two 'masterminds' behind the recent cases of hacking. The matter was now closed.

However, the cops were unaware of the fact that Hakim had just murdered three students and buried their bodies. Afraid of being pinned as an accomplice in the murder, Qadir had stayed quiet. The matter did not come up again until questions were asked about the last hack involving Mr. Abbasi's bank account. Irfan had already confessed to having no part in that attack and the police already knew that Hakim was incapable of doing this on his own, which could only mean that there was a second unknown accomplice unaccounted for. The police ran around, trying to pin down who this person could be.

There was no one amongst Hakim's known accomplices with this kind of skill set. They would have had to go to an expert to get through this level of security. There were very few people in the country capable of such a feat, all who had rock-solid alibi for the time of the attack. The task force was not allowed to disband until the last accomplice was caught. He needed to see this to its end, or he and all his men would be unable to move on, not just because they would be stuck in the task force but also because they would be unable to rest easy.

***

One Week Later

"Come now, man! Just tell us who the other man was! I already told you the prosecutor give you a lighter sentence if you just give us a name, we're not asking you for an address or location all I want is a name that isn't so hard to give. is it?" Lal Zaman had lost his patience with this man, asking him the same questions for a week now, Qadir wasn't saying a word. He wasn't even giving information on how the targets were selected, what the criteria was or the prerequisites.

Lal Zaman had had it up to here now. He was ready to chuck the guy out the window, it wouldn't be hard, you could just say it was an accident, or the man was suicidal, there were so many possibilities. He wouldn't do it, of course, what do you like to think about it. It gave him a perverse kind of pleasure.

He got a call on his cell phone. "...Bodies? Why do I care three bodies? What do you mean they're connected to my case? I run a cybercrime unit... We don't do dead bodies, contact homicide." He was about to hang up, "Wait, say that again, they were all tech students, and they've been dead about a week? Are you sure? Positive. Okay, I'll be right there." He stared at Qadir. "Well, well, well, now I know why you wouldn't tell me who that accomplice was, it's because they are dead."

Qadir broke down into hysterics leaving Lal Zaman looking shocked. *Well, you certainly don't see that every day.*

In a broken voice, he had confessed to everything. He told Lal how Hakim had paid a boy named Jamal to start a fight with another boy called Ahmed, who was well known for being an expert hacker on campus.

"Hakim basically took the boy under his wing. The kid, Ahmed, well, he was looking for someone to approve of all the stuff that he had been doing." He continued to tell Lal the whole sordid tale.

Every time Qadir stopped, and it was often, he would look around in the interrogation room, which was dark except for the pendant light above the interrogation table. The room was veiled in shadows. Qadir glanced around as if he expected Hakim to jump out from the darkness and stab him to death or something.

Lal was being patient. He wanted to tie up all and any loose ends so that the case could be closed. Legally, he could only ask Qadir questions for a limited number of hours a day. At the pace that the bastard was talking, it might take him a few days to coax all the information out of him. He looked like he had lost his mind a little bit.

Lal wondered if it was from witnessing the violence with which Hakim had acted, which did not sound probable either because the man was a violent criminal himself and had done plenty of truly horrible things over the years. Lal doubted he was going to try for an insanity plea, with his record no one would ever believe that he had suddenly become mad. Lal would take his time if he had to, but he would get all the information from this man, even if he had to use less than legal means to obtain it. Lal was aware that there were methods of 'interrogating' people that would prompt them to talk and would not leave any evidence. Lal knew more than one man in his precinct who was more than adept at using those 'interrogation' techniques and had no problem at all applying them.

***

On an Unnamed Island

Hakim had finally done it. He had outsmarted everyone. Now he was in the middle of the Pacific Ocean on an island owned by a country that had no extradition treaty with Pakistan and was willing to take his money in exchange for keeping his location a secret.

As he lay on the beach, Hakim took that time to admire the island around him.

He let the memory of the night he had killed that idiot Ahmed, and his unlucky friends fill him. He recalled the pleasure he had felt at watching the life drain from their eyes. He could live off that feeling for a while, but he would need to kill soon. Perhaps the local islanders could be persuaded to look the other way if the occasional man or woman disappeared once or twice a year.

Hakim could sustain his hunger, and he would be more than satisfied to spend the rest of his life a freeman on this rather beautiful jewel of an island.

As he lay on his back, he noticed a young couple walking hand and hand laughing as they touched their feet. Now that was an enticing sight. They looked like tourists, and with how remote the island was, it might be awhile before anyone noticed they were missing. By then, Hakim would have disposed of the bodies correctly. In fact, he had found just the place to stash them.

He had lost his little retreat because he had to move; however, it wouldn't take very long to fill his new cave with the wonders and trophies that he would collect from his victims. With a smile, he began to walk toward the couple, a plan already forming in his mind.

***

A Few Days Later

Hinna Azan had not slept for days. She had taken pills, alcohol, and the prompting of an old friend some herbal infusions to call sleep to her. It had not helped at all. Her baby girl had not come home. Hinna was not going to sleep until she had her girl back with her.

She got a call. When she hung up the phone, her heart was no longer in her chest. The cavity felt empty. There was no beat. She made no sound as she went upstairs and turned her bath on and waited for it to fill.

This was not a decision that she was making lightly, long ago when her husband had died, she had decided to take her life on the off chance that something ever happened to her daughter. It had happened. The unthinkable had occurred. For years she had never considered the possibility that her daughter would pass before her. As any parent would, she had indulged in the fantasy of seeing her child happy, married, and perhaps with her own children and a family.

This what's wrong. It went against the laws of nature for parents to outlive their children, it shouldn't happen, but it had.

Hinna was unharmed, while her child lay dead. How was such an atrocity possible? The true reality of what happened smacked her in the face.

The white bathroom tiles were pristine. For a moment, Hinna regretted the mess that it would make when she finally did the deed. It was a rather silly thought to have in a moment like this. Then again, it didn't matter what mess she left behind because this house is no longer a home, just an empty shell of brick and mortar. A home was made of the people who lived in it, and now the occupants were gone.

The silence in the house was so loud she felt like she was going to go mad. When the bath was half full, she climbed in, completely dressed. Hinna reached for the razor on the edge of the bath and slowly with deliberate movements, sliced her wrist. She cut at the base of her wrist at least five inches up her arm. She followed the same path on her right hand; it was harder with her left hand, the cut was less deep, but it was equally long.

She let the razor slip from her hand, her hands were slick with ruby liquid, she didn't see where it fell, she did not care. Almost reverently she lowered her arms into the bath. She knew that this was wrong. It was weak, but the truth was she had no reason to live anymore.

Her reason to do anything had been her daughter. She had meant everything to her. Without Liyana, Hinna had nothing. No purpose, no goal; nothing to live for. She closed her eyes slipping into the cool comforting darkness. She would follow her daughter into that otherworld. She hoped that God would forgive her. She hoped that He would understand why she did what she did. The darkness closed in around her and she didn't fight it, she let it come over her.

As she drifted into the darkness, she felt consoled by a small measure that her daughter might be on the other side. She did believe in God and hoped that He would grant her dying plea and allow her to see her daughter, even if it were just for a single moment -- if only to know that she was safe. Those were her last thoughts as the darkness overwhelmed her for the last time.

She could finally sleep.

Chapter Twelve

The bodies were found near the banks of the Ravi River. The three youngsters had been buried in shallow graves, dug rather quickly, and messily by whoever was covering the bodies up. Soon the whole city was abuzz with rumors about what had happened. No one quite knew the entire story; some thought was a lovers' spat gone wrong.

Others thought it was a drug-related death.

Some even believed that it was a cult suicide. This was perhaps the strangest and most bizarre rumour going around; it was so far from the truth that it was improbable. It was well into autumn when all the pieces finally fell into place.

The campus was abuzz with rumors about what had happened last in the last few months. Three students, all well-known and mostly well-liked around campus had gone missing. The events around the disappearances were jumbled, and no two stories about what really happened seamed to line up.

What was even more of a mystery was the death of a rather popular professor, Hinna Azan. Her death and the circumstances had been swept under a rug. No one was being told how she died or even why it happened. The reason this news was so demanded was because she had been the mother of one of the students who had gone missing. The fact that she died soon after was rather suspicious. Most people suspected some kind of foul play. No one outside her immediate family was aware of the fact that the professor had committed suicide. They had bribed a police officer to help falsify her death certificate as an accident so that she could get a proper burial.

The air was chilly, and a light morning fog covered the wide campus grounds and parking lots. The air smelled vaguely of flowers, mostly roses with a hint of jasmine. The campus roads were lined with Evergreen shrubbery, trimmed to perfection in Boxwood hedges, and the occasional hidden figurine that the campus groundsman had cut had in a moment of impulsiveness.

The autumn leaves danced as the light cool breeze swept them up into small tornadoes and the tumbled along the brick-paved walkways. The last of the summer flowers lingered around as the change in season turning everything toward the shades of autumn. The greens, of spring and summer, gave way to the bright reds, oranges, golds, and yellows of autumn. A few stray leaves held on stubbornly to their summer colours as everything around them embraced the coming of autumn and the change of season.

The lovely picture the campus presented, stood in stark juxtaposition against the general mood around campus. People in every corner could be seen whispering, talking about the events that had taken place just weeks earlier. The buzz and chatter of the students were almost deafening.

Everyone seemed to be talking about the same thing -- what had happened to Ahmed, Adnan, and Liyana. The details were obscure, in fact, the exact events were an unknown factor as well. The only thing that could be agreed upon was that all three of the students had met a rather unfortunate fate at the same time. The three best friends had been missing for a week now, and no one, not even their families, seemed to know what had happened to them. Few people knew the truth, mostly because initially the police didn't want the news aired that banks had been compromised all accounts. So, the story stayed hush-hush.

The families of the deceased were told the truth, or at least the version of the truth that the police have been able to gather. It was hardly the real truth, but no truth would bring comfort to those who had lost loved ones.

It's certainly brought no comfort to the grieving mothers of those three youngsters. It brought no comfort to their friends, to the people that loved them, and the people that had been loved by them. It was a tragedy like no other.

Lal Zaman was one of the few people who knew the whole truth. He had helped forge the certificates of death for both the Azan women. He and his unit also had the unfortunate task of informing the families of the deceased children that the bodies had been found and identified. Lal had been a police officer for a long time now, and telling families that their children, their loved ones, or their spouses had been found dead was something that he believed would never get easier. He recalled each family's reaction to the news of their deaths. Unfortunately, not all the families had been informed by the police directly.

The mother of Liyana Azan had received the news through a call from a friend who worked at one of the precincts in the city. The call had been well intended; however, this news was best given in person. The unfortunate method of delivery had meant that no one was there to console her upon receiving the news, and in a state of uncontrollable grief, the woman had taken her life. She had slipped into her room and slit her wrists in the bath. By the time the extended family had received the news and arrived at the house, she had already been dead for several hours.

Lal had been present for the other two family's notifications. He had watched as the couples had collapsed upon receiving the news. Three bright young lives snuffed out much too early, seemingly without cause or provocation.

Such was the way with life, things happen

unexpectedly, and one could hardly brace for what was unknown. Lal Zaman was not sure what he had expected when he first taken this case. He certainly had not expected for it to end with all these deaths. No one had told him that he would have to tell three mothers that their children were gone from this world.

He had not expected to have to tell fathers their sons were gone. This was supposed to be a simple case involving a bunch of hackers. What was the purpose of everything that had happened? It did not make sense.

The bright morning sunlight mocked them on such a grievous occasion. It was a beautiful day. Lal Zaman always hated it when the weather at a funeral was bright and pleasant, without a single dark cloud to mark the sad occasion. The lack on overcast on this day really did feel as if the heavens where mocking them.

Lal Zaman was a man of faith. He went to the mosque and stayed away from vices like gambling and alcohol, he was not a thief and minus the occasional white lie to superior about a report that he had written. Lal Was not in the habit deception, without a purpose. Even the bribes that he took were taken from people who could afford it and he hadn't really committed a crime that warranted severe legal action. Yet, for the life of him, Lal could not make sense of what it just happened. Three young lives had simply been snuffed out because one madman had decided that was the only way he would get what was his.

Hakim was nowhere to be found; he had not left any trace of his presence behind at the scene. The only proof that they had was some blood found under the fingernails of one victim. The girl had managed to scratch him, and the presence of his blood was the only
thing that linked him to the scene, other than Qadir's Rather wonky and unreliable testimony of the events. They had his DNA on file and were able to match it.

However, the problem came from the fact that despite having his DNA on file, clear testimony that he had been at the scene, and evidence from multiple witnesses who had seen Ahmed and Hakim together on various occasions, the truth was they had nothing. This was the cause Hakim was in the wind, they did not know where he was when he would get back or how they would find him again. The man had disappeared without a trace of any kind.

All of his acquaintances, friends, and family were

dragged into the interrogation rooms and questioned over and over again for any information They couldn't provide about his whereabouts. Unfortunately, they had been of no help to the police.

Lal was now stuck. He had no answers to all the questions that ran through his head. Without Hakim, he would never find the answers. Lal watched as they lowered the bodies of the kids into the freshly dug graves in the cemetery. The families of the children had decided to bury them close to each other. Lal wasn't sure what good that would do, but it seemed to bring them comfort to know that their children would be together, even if it were only in the afterlife.

As Lal Looked around the graveyard, he saw the families of the children gathered; he was quite aware of the fact that Hinna Azan had committed suicide upon learning of her daughter's death. As the death had been discovered as a suicide, she was not allowed to be buried in the cemetery near a mosque. Instead, her family purchased a small plot just outside the cemetery and buried here there just yesterday while they waited to receive the body of their granddaughter from the police and hold her funeral the next day. That family was crushed. They probably would never recover from this. Life was hard enough without having to deal with so much death and sadness.

Truth be told, Lal's faith had seriously been shaken by the events that had taken place over the last few months. It was hard to believe that someone could do such horrible things over money. He had been a cop for more than two decades now and witnessed some of the worst acts of humanity, but it always held firm to the belief that all things had a bigger purpose in the tapestry of the order of the world.

Today he didn't feel that way. Today he felt hopeless and lost. It would be a long time before he was able to get up in the morning and not think of what had been done to these children. He didn't even want to think about the fact that with Hakim still out there on the loose, there might be more children used, manipulated, and then in all likelihood be killed.

This man was a monster. Lal vowed that he would catch him and bring him to justice, even if he had to spend the rest of his future at the police department working for the cybercrime division. It suddenly struck him as ironic that he was willing to spend the rest of his life doing this job even though just months ago, he had resented his superiors for placing him in this department. Ironic that things changed so quickly, because of circumstances and time and so many other factors.

As the funeral prayer ended, Lal had come to a decision. He Would find this man. He already had a plan forming in his mind for how he would track trace and finally trap this insidious monster once and for all.

Let the chase begin. *I'm coming for you.*

***

On an Unnamed Island – Two Years Later

As Hakim lay down, admiring his surroundings, the wind kissed his skin as he enjoyed the drink in his hand. He admired the island; the white sand beach felt warm between his toes as he looked up to the crystal blue sky. A smirk held onto his face. He got up and walked toward his mansion; however, he slowed his track to admire the giant palm trees that created shade their beautiful white bark shot up and stood tall while the wind blew its leaves. The crystal blue and green water glistened as the sun rays touched it, creating a beautiful effect. As he slowly approached the path that led toward his home, more trees filled his vision.

The path which was made of a beautiful cobblestone

trail shaded by the trees at the entrance of his house. Light was bright by day, but at night time, it could get dark; hence why he had lights to illuminate his way along the track. It took only a few more steps, and he was at his grand entrance.

His guards stood toward the side speaking in their native language; it was one he did not speak, but had every intention of learning -- one could never be too careful. His personal guard was always beside him hiding in the background, but always present, never leaving his side, which was a constant reminder of the crimes he committed. He didn't have any guilt at all, and he didn't realise his inner monologue had made him stop short in his tracks alarming the guard beside him.

"Anything wrong, sir?" Vladimir spoke in a hushed tone, and although his tone sounded concerned, his emotionless face spoke to the contrary.

"No, I was just thinking," Hakim replied in a nonchalant tone. He continued walking as he opened his door to his safe-haven; a white grand staircase was the first thing that he saw when he walked in. He slowly moved toward his den while Vladimir and his other guards walked toward their office located right.

A giant 72-inch flat screen covered one wall, and the other was a glass ceiling that opened up to the courtyard that was decorated with plants and a large grey cloud couch that could house at least eight people, then again, he had no one to share this with.

He slumped his body on the white cloud couch located inside the den. Right behind him was a console that had a few pictures of his family, all of whom where long gone and buried. He looked at a picture of his beautiful mother, the only person who he remotely showed any emotion.

"You would have loved it here *Ami*," he spoke in his native Urdu which he rarely did anymore, since retreating to this island. Moments like this had him think he might have some humanity left, but then he would have murderous thoughts and realized that any humanity that he had left was finished when he had committed murder.

He put his feet on the ottoman that was placed in front of the couch. He lazily reached for the remote on the end table and turned on the television to watch the news. CNN was on, and they were discussing a new trade deal established by the United States of America and the Islamic Republic of

Pakistan; this made him think about investing some of his money into some legal fronts to make more profit.

He admired his house. He had paid a world-renowned architect to construct his home. Hakim wanted a modern, sleek home that very much showed off his wealth. Money that he didn't have when he was growing up in the slums of Pakistan.

He slowly got up as the news had now bored him, no longer caring about the success his former country was having. He walked toward his bedroom taking the staircase to the upper level of his mansion the more private area, an area where he would plan his next job. With rather deliberate slow steps he walked toward the master bedroom, his room, he opened the door and remembered to lock it after him.

He slumped on his bed and made a loud noise of frustration; nothing was amusing him anymore. He wanted to have fun again, to do something risky. He would have to ponder on that more. At a leisurely pace, he made his way to the balcony; however, a loud noise made him stop; it was his stomach; it was rumbling, begging to be fed.

Only then did he realise that it was way past

lunchtime. Strolling to the intercom, he pressed the call button and spoke, "Vladimir, ask someone to bring me something to eat."

"Yes sir!" came the quick reply from his henchmen, Hakim rarely spoke to anyone other than his personal bodyguard. Completing his walk toward his balcony, he stood on his balcony that overlooked the ocean, the sun was slowly setting, but its majestic beauty almost enchanting. A knock pulled him out of his thoughts; his food had arrived, freshly made as always, his workers feared him and thrived on pleasing him.

He finished his food and continued to admire his island until nightfall. He decided to call it a day and go to sleep. He walked over to his bed and got in turning off the light. The darkness came upon him. In the moments before he fell asleep, he remembered he had a 'guest' in the basement. Over the last couple of years, once or twice a year he would have a 'guest' and the locals were more than willing to overlook his indiscretion.

He would keep them around until he grew bored. This time he had become bored much too quickly. Maybe it was time to return to the mainland for a short excursion. He could use the distraction. It would be fun to wreak some havoc on the unsuspecting people who he would undoubtedly come across.

Decision made, he let the darkness embrace him all the way -- the dark pit of sleep a welcoming refuge for his rapidly moving brain.

The End

ABOUT THE AUTHOR

 Hassan Asghar Bhatti belongs to a political family in Pakistan.
He studied law in the UK and has been an avid reader since childhood.

The 31 years old is the author of the debut book "As the Heavens Smiled." He has been involved in some researches recently.

Hassan has written some other publications, and he is an enthusiastic person whose bookworm nature earned him his status today. The "Fate" is another of his publications, and it aims to satisfy a lot in the minds of the readers.

Hassan has a lot of experiences and exposure, even at this early stage of life, because he loves to read, travel, and acquire knowledge in its full abundance.

As a lawyer, he works to serve the justice he believes in. He has a brand to his name, and you can find some of his creative works here.

Hassan Asghar Bhatti

www.ingramcontent.com/pod-product-compliance
Lightning Source LLC
Chambersburg PA
CBHW070920130626
46555CB00001B/219